I0530746

Unwed & Dead

The Dead Ex Files – Book 1

Claire Kane & Stan Crowe

Breezy Reads

ISBN-13: 978-1-938327-22-3

ONE

Victor St. John cautiously stepped into his Tokyo apartment, keeping the grocery bag he held concealed behind him. "Lacey?" he called. "Jessica?"

It was dark. For a moment, he had the impression that one of them was just inside, waiting for him, perhaps even planning a surprise. At least he'd given Lacey a spare set of keys. Jessica, on the other hand...

He flicked on the light and found everything in order. A wary search of the hall and his bedroom, also revealed nothing.

"Hello?" Still no response. Good. He sighed in relief, then smiled, making his way around the stacks of moving boxes that covered the living room's hardwood floor to the kitchen where he'd put the rest of his plan into motion. He set his bag on the counter and got to work.

Gently, he emptied its contents: a pair of the best steaks he could find—he could have bought an entire cow in America for what he paid for them—a bottle of wine that would make his parents jealous, and a nice little rock on an engagement band. Forward much? Sure, but maybe if Lacey knew just *how* committed he was, she'd change her mind. Victor St. John was a man on a mission. He swallowed again at the cost of the evening, but Lacey Ling was worth it.

He paused at a snifter poised on the counter, a healthy dose of dark red liquid already leaving a ring around the inside of the glass. Next to it was a note, written in kanji. Taking the glass in one hand, and the note in the other, Victor read what Lacey had left for him. "To you, my love," he said, automatically translating from Japanese.

His heart stopped. Had she really written this? If so, when? And why wasn't she still in the apartment? He smiled, thinking that maybe she'd stepped out to get something comfortable to wear to dinner. Had all the time they'd spent apart broken that glacier that formed between them? It had been six weeks since she dumped him. Maybe she just needed time to reconsider. Stomach flopping like a fish, his spirits soared. Tonight's plan might actually work.

"Well," he said to himself, "can't let the little lady down, can I?" He swirled the liquid, sniffed lightly—not a bad scent, but not the best he'd ever encountered—and sipped at it. It was lukewarm, and a tad on the bitter side, but not bad enough to not finish. He knew she'd be upset if he rejected the offer, so he downed it in a long gulp, then wiped his mouth.

He grimaced at the taste. "Yeah. I should have taught her where to shop for wine," he muttered, before taking his own bottle and setting it in the freezer to ensure it was properly chilled before what he was sure would be the best dinner they'd ever had.

He turned to the stove, set out a pan, and pulled out his phone, where he'd bookmarked a recipe his boss, Mister Taniguchi, had highly recommended. Pulling some cooking sherry from the tiny cupboard (he'd never gotten over how much the Japanese spent on such minuscule living spaces), he unscrewed the lid, and poured a little into a pan while turning on the gas burner. (He felt lucky to have found a place that had one).

A thud sounded in the next apartment over, causing him to start, but with a shake of his head, he turned on some tunes and lost himself in his cooking. Knowing Lacey, she'd arrive half an hour before he'd asked her to, and want to take over the cooking, at which point, the game would be up. He felt lucky that she'd left after leaving a note.

Victor sighed, and checked his watch. "Best get a move on, Vic," he muttered, grabbing a cutting board and a knife, before pulling some fresh garlic cloves from the fridge. As he shut the door, he felt his head swim a little. Blinking through the dizziness, he turned back to the counter to start cutting the garlic, only to feel an unexpected wave of nausea rip through his gut. "Ugh. That sushi joint last night must have gotten it wrong." A cold sweat broke on his forehead, and he had to catch himself with both hands to keep from dropping. After a few moments, though, the sensation seemed to pass, and he made his way unsteadily to the sink for a glass of water, dismayed to note that his vision was blurring rapidly.

What is going on?

He nursed the headache rising in his temples. "Never going to finish in time if I keep feeling this way."

Draining the water in one, long gulp, he moved back to the cutting board and picked up the knife. His clouded vision hampered his efforts to mince the garlic and but he pressed on, taking extra care not to leave a finger in the small-but-growing pile of chopped produce, and wondered how much his old college girlfriend, Jessica, would laugh if he did. *Geez*, he thought, *she'd probably offer to help.* He shuddered to think of how close he'd gotten to making things permanent with her. But Lacey—she was different. She was the real deal.

He heard a noise again, only this time he realized it was from his living room. *I'm more out of it than I thought if she snuck in like that*. He looked up slowly, careful not to agitate his headache again. Oddly, the light had been switched off. "Lacey? That you?" Wiping the knife clean, he half stumbled out of the kitchen, wondering what kind of surprise she had in store for him.

"Lacey?" he said, flipping on the light.

Pain erupted in the side of his face. Before he could react, a hand snatched his collar and hurled him to the floor. He gasped—half from shock—and arched his back. A fist piled into the back of his head, and a kick forced him to curl into a ball. He rolled out of the way, and managed to get halfway up before another kick blasted him. By pure instinct, Victor's knife lashed out, and his attacker hissed in pain.

Desperately he struggled in vain to clear his vision. In the darkness of the living room, all he could see was a black, vaguely human blob retreating from where he held the knife. Victor backed into the kitchen, still waving the knife in front of him. When his attacker lunged, Victor fell back on his military martial arts training. He tried to block and thrust, but the intruder dodged, and drove a knee into his groin before grabbing for the knife. His stomach still roiled, and his head felt like it was caught in a tornado, but he knew that losing the knife meant only one thing—that he wouldn't be eating dinner with Lacey that night.

Her face appeared in his addled mind, and with a roar, he heaved his attacker off him and drove the man into the wall. He earned a punch for his efforts, and Victor staggered back into the stove, sending the pan skittering off the burner and on to the floor. The bottle of sherry was knocked sideways, where it sullenly bled out on to the stovetop.

Waves of pain and vertigo crashed in on Victor at the same time the burglar did. Victor went down hard, and dropped the knife. Both grabbed for it at the same time, but by some miracle, Victor's hand found it first even as the man was diving for it. Like lightning, Victor whipped it up, and heard a sickly, wet tearing sound followed by a gurgling scream as his attacker collapsed on to him. Instinctively, he twisted the knife, but could already feel his grip slipping. His vision clouded around the edges, and he vomited. Any advantage he may have had had just disappeared.

And then the weight was off him. Frantic footsteps retreated into the hall. Whatever Victor had done, it had been enough. He'd rest for a minute—his body refused to let him do much more— then he'd phone the cops. Explaining this to Lacey was a different matter.

I paid a lot of money for those steaks, too. His stomach violently protested the idea of ingesting half-raw meat, and he threw up again. Head pounding, and breath shallow, he only managed to look up at the counter one more time before sliding into the billowing grey clouds closing in around his vision.

His last thought was to wonder what the flames on his counter were about.

*

The local news, that night, would include the usual things—typhoon recovery, economic reports, tensions in the South China Sea, and a fire that gutted a high-rise apartment in Tokyo, leaving the charred husk of a single victim, and scant few clues as to why it happened.

TWO

The quiet, incessant ticking of a clock pressed on Lacey Ling's mind as she sat in the semi-dark of her grandmother's tiny home on the outskirts of Tokyo. The scent of "old woman" seemed to weigh on the air, as if her mother's mother's life was breathing a final sigh before letting go. Lacey had come to Tokyo on company business, and decided to take the opportunity to present a proposal to the aged woman. Instead, the conversation had, inevitably, turned back on Lacey and toward her continued singlehood. She cringed, but humored her, out of respect for her elder.

"Nainai," Lacey said, stroking her grandmother's whitened hair, "I'm just not ready to commit, and especially not to him."

Nainai peered up at her through pink eyelids, lying in a bed of multicolored silks. "He is stable. He has a job; a good one at that. And he would give you a handsome son."

"We've only known each other a few months, Nainai!" Lacey shook her head in frustration, long black bangs framing her oval face.

"Your grandfather and I didn't know each other before

our wedding day! Five months is plenty of time. Plus, he's an American." A wrinkled finger pointed up in emphasis.

"I'm an American too. Chinese-American, no disrespect. There are plenty of men back home in the States, all around, I can have a chance with."

A hacking cough started. Nainai cupped her mouth and closed her eyes.

"I'm sorry, you need to rest. I shouldn't be talking to you about this." Lacey stood up from her antique, stuffed chair.

The elderly Chinese woman pushed herself up into a sitting position. "I'm not dead yet! Let me tell you what Confucius says—" Her dark eyes were focused with excitement.

"Oh, no. Not Confucius again, Nainai." Lacey put a hand on her hip.

"Confucius say, 'You are a pretty girl, but not always smart!'"

A sigh. "He eats Lucky Charms while watching Godzilla on repeat, likes Christian rock… *and* I have proof he sometimes wears the same socks two days in a row!"

"Not two days in a row." Nainai pressed a hand against her blouse in dramatized shock. "Look, I know you American girls marry for love. That's fine. It's what your mother did. I just know there's something about Victor that's different. He has a spiritual side. He's a person you can depend on."

Lacey's expression stayed flat.

"But you don't love him?"

"We had a whirlwind romance, as you know. I couldn't get enough of him… until suddenly one day I did. I'll put it this way: he doesn't have the maturity I'm seeking. His boyishness can only be cute for so long. Plus, we're too different. It could never work out."

"So you don't love him."

Lacey looked away. "Not like that."

Nainai slowly reclined and shut her eyes. "I won't push you further. That is that. Pass me my dim sum."

Lacey placed the ornate saucer of ornate snacks in bed, then kissed her grandma's forehead. "Um, Nainai, I have something to talk to you about, other than Victor."

Nainai took a bite of a small steamed bun stuffed with pork. "Go on."

"I talked to Mom, and she agrees, you should come home with me to live back in the States."

"Now why would I do that?" Her eyes narrowed. "Leave my home that I and your late grandfather made? Those drapes were handsewn by me at just seventeen years old. That chair you sit on goes back to the Ming Dynasty. I have memories here."

"I agree, there are items here of great value, but what's most important right now is that I care for you. I can come back for many of these things. You don't want to be here all alone, do you? Your family isn't here; it's where I'm at."

The old woman's forehead wrinkled as she took another bite. "Hmmmm."

"Come on. Confucius say, 'You should do it.'" Lacey winked.

"You can't use my lines!" she joked. "I'll think about it…"

"Goodnight." Lacey grabbed a black oversized purse off the floor, and put it over a shoulder. "I'll be back later." Though Nainai hadn't committed, Lacey could tell she was thinking about it; that meant Lacey probably wouldn't have to cancel the one-way ticket she'd already bought her grandmother. With her primary task complete, she turned her mind to the next thing on her list: her ex. She sighed, but straightened her hair all the same as she hailed a cab for a ride into the city.

*

Soon enough, Tokyo's city lights of loud neon billboards and towering buildings were Lacey's backdrop. Colorful, crowded advertisements in Japanese couldn't lure her into their tourist traps, however, as she stepped out of the cab, nearly a block away from her destination. Glancing at her Apple watch, she noted she was fashionably late for her appointment with Victor. She would've rather been early, but the cab hit delays on the ride from Nainai's, and with traffic gridlocked near Victor's apartment, she reasoned it was probably easier to walk the rest of the way, even in her $120 shoes.

She sighed. Victor had invited her to his place on the excuse of "some final business over dinner." He insisted she come, as he was set to fly out tomorrow morning. Though she saw through his act, she'd decided to be a good friend and help, even if part of her was looking forward to saying goodbye.

The streets were wet from a recent rainfall. Puddles reflected reds, blues and pinks, appearing like giant ink splotches. Lacey's tall beige heels cautiously clacked along, as she wove through businessmen, college students and an occasional prostitute or two. Ahead, she saw the flashing lights of emergency vehicles. She ignored it and peeked inside her purse. Wrapped in butcher paper were two steaks side by side. If Victor had to choose, Lacey was certain he'd pick her cooking. She was a natural at it. Victor tried making steak for her before. She asked for rare; it was past well done. She wouldn't let that mistake happen again. No, she would see to it that nothing was burnt tonight.

*

High above Lacey's frustration, Victor woke to the sight of his apartment looking like the aftermath of a volcanic eruption, and a bad house party composed of Japanese firefighters and police traipsing through puddles of water.

When had Lacey invited these guys? And what happened to the guy who had attacked him? Is that who was on the sheet-covered stretcher out in his damaged hallway?

I guess I stabbed him deeper than I meant to. Geez. I wasn't trying to kill the guy. He shouldn't have come for me in the first place.

Victor stood with surprising ease and no longer felt the slightest bit drowsy. His nausea, headache, and dizziness were gone too. In fact, he felt absolutely *superb*. There was a strange sensation that he'd lost some weight while he was unconscious, but hey, that wasn't necessarily a bad thing, as long as it wasn't the muscle mass he'd been building over the last year.

Turning in a slow circle, he noticed that the firemen—who were practically crawling all over his apartment—were in full gear. It only took a split second's thought to remember that he'd seen flames before he'd blacked out. Suddenly, he was glad they'd come.

"Hey," he called. "How'd you guys get here so fast?" But that didn't seem right. The charred walls, the piles of ash and melted plastic where his furniture once were didn't speak to a speedy arrival. As it was, they continued swarming the place, clearly too busy to answer, carrying on as though he hadn't said a word. Standing in the middle of the unmitigated disaster, Victor knew that *someone* had some explaining to do. Then, something else hit him. One look at the stove made his heart sink. "Lacey likes her steak rare. She's never going to forgive this."

Wait a sec, he thought. *I just got attacked in my own apartment, which is now torched, and I'm worried about* steaks? *Wow. But hey. It's for Lacey. I can always get a new apartment.*

Sighing, he skirted the island counter and waved at a firefighter heading in his direction. "Hey. Konnichiwa, dude. Care to tell me why you didn't RSVP? And sorry, I don't know how to say that in Japanese." The uniformed man moved by with a purpose, neither stopping nor even trying to dodge Victor. So Victor dodged him.

Something felt off. He'd been standing right next to the island when he'd sidestepped his unwelcome company. He looked down toward the counter and immediately wished he hadn't. The counter was protruding halfway through his torso, and he couldn't feel a thing. He felt his breath catch—only there was no breath to catch. He closed his eyes and slowly placed his fingers on the inside of his wrist.

Nothing.

Victor froze. The implications seeped into his mind. Barely daring, he willed himself over to the stretcher, and no one stopped him. He reached for the sheet, only to have his hand pass right through it. He tried again with the same results. And a third time. He tensed in frustration, grinding his teeth. "Can someone please move this sheet for me?"

Almost as if he had heard him, a police officer stepped out into the hall, a camera dangling from his neck, and a clipboard in one hand. The officer readied his camera, then lifted the sheet. As the flash exploded, Victor saw the worst thing he'd ever seen in his life.

Himself. Face blackened, half melted, and not at all ready to greet his future wife.

"Aww *man*," he exclaimed, falling back against a wall, only to fall through it into the apartment next door. He stumbled to right himself, and found himself upright as soon as the thought occurred to him. "What is going *on*?"

In reply, a cold whisper whisked through his mind.

"Hello?"

The whisper came again, but if someone was saying something, he couldn't understand it. Suddenly remembering he was in his neighbor's living room, he looked around frantically to see whether he had interrupted anything. Thankfully, the room was empty, and as sodden as the charred husk of his own digs.

Legion.

He paused at the nearly imperceptible word. In fact, it was almost more a feeling than anything he'd actually heard.

11

Ignoring it, he strode to the door and reached for the handle, only to pass right through it. "So why am I not falling through the *floor*?" He asked to no one in particular. "You've *got* to be kidding me. I *can't* be dead. I've got a killer date planned for Lacey. This *can't* be happening."

Legion.

The hairs on his neck rose. *Great. I'm dead, but I can still freak out. That's just wonderful.* A sense of cold dread began pecking at the outer edges of his thoughts. He ignored it again and, forcing a sigh for the sake of it, he walked through the door—eyes closed—and back into the hall. Two medical technicians were wheeling the stretcher into the elevator at the end of the hall, and he ran to catch up. The doors slid closed too soon, and he cursed himself for not being in the elevator.

So he closed his eyes again and simply charged through.

Settling in between the medtechs, he waited as the elevator descended, still wondering why he wasn't just falling to the center of the earth. "Okay, this is really starting to trip me out now." The medical techs didn't seem to notice his comment, but carried on a muttered conversation in Japanese. After a few moments, Victor realized that he could understand them, despite his general lack of language skills.

"They are lucky the entire building didn't burn down," one man said. Instantly, Victor knew—the way people know in dreams—the man's name, and everything about his life. Father of one, married for five years but cheating on his wife with four different women. In heavy debt to the local yakuza, and a bit too fond of saké and gambling.

"Stupid American," the second tech said. "He probably got drunk and lit the place on fire just to show how amazing he thought he was. He probably tried to put it out by urinating on it. Maybe he thought he would be better at it than the fire sprinklers." Both men laughed. As with the first tech, the full bio of the second guy practically appeared before Victor's eyes. College kid in med school. Never had a girlfriend. Lived with his parents and played games in his free time. Still held a grudge against the US for Hiroshima and Nagasaki.

"Hey!" Victor called. "Watch it."

The techs both paused momentarily. Drunken Cheater glanced around. Gamer Boy looked momentarily confused.

"Wait," Victor said. "Can you guys actually hear me?" He waved his hand in front of their faces. "Hello? Konnichiwa? Ohayō?" The techs both shrugged, and carried on, though Gamer Boy didn't make any more snarky comments about Americans all the way down to the lobby.

Victor followed them out into the street, and toward the waiting ambulance. He was about to climb in when the creepy voice/feeling thing buzzed through him again.

Legion!

They were there without further warning. Scores of vague black shapes surrounding the ambulance and spilling across the sidewalk in front of his apartment building. They seemed to absorb the harsh glare of streetlights. Victor froze, unable to resist watching them. It didn't take long for him to realize that the shapes were more than just that— they were people.

I'm guessing they're the leftover of Soylent Green…

His eyes were somehow able to track them all simultaneously. And then he made out their faces, and immediately wished he hadn't. Hideously twisted masks of hatred, extreme hunger, and envy were everywhere he looked.

"My… gosh," he whispered.

Across the street, he saw a swarm of the things crowding around a local bar and brothel. As soon as he thought of the place, he found himself inside, peering through thin curtains of opium haze and cigarette smoke that diffused the dim neon from the bar. The place looked surprisingly American. The shadowy beings were packed in the place like sardines, every one of them scrabbling with wicked claws at the various patrons, as though they could somehow rip them open. A small fight erupted in one of the back booths, and the shadows were so thick there he could hardly even see the men who were throwing punches. Lisping, sinister choruses of laughter hissed from the men, even though their lips weren't moving. All at once, Victor knew the brawlers were no longer in control of their own bodies. When one man finally went down, a demon emerged from the fallen man, its dark eyes mingled with despair and ecstasy.

Legion!

Victor turned and bolted for the door, dodging tables, chairs and the handful of patrons still on their feet. Bursting into the open night air, he ran for the ambulance, which was already pulling away. A sinking feeling alerted him to the notion that his sudden flight must have attracted unwanted attention.

Legion. The word drew out long and slow in his mind, and he felt cold.

The creatures materialized between him and the ambulance that was taking his body away. Then they were on his right hand and his left. Victor whirled back toward his apartment building, only to find they were there, too. He could even feel them in the air above him.

Legion.

Waving his arms frantically, he tried batting the vaporous forms away, but to no avail. "Seriously, get lost!"

No flesh. They hissed as one. *Just like us, now.*

"I am *not* like you! I've got a hot girlfriend who's going to marry me once I can quit being dead. Now *leave me alone!*"

In an instant, they were swarming around him. The lights around him blurred, and so very dim. He felt as though his heart should be bursting, but remembered he still had no pulse. The creatures continued to suck every shred of warmth from him, and he felt as though an invisible cage was closing on him, trapping him; shrinking him. Victor's will to exist was dying at an accelerating pace.

Lacey! Lacey! he cried in his mind. *Help me, babe! Someone, please!*

THREE

Rounding the corner of Victor's apartment building, Lacey realized that part of her didn't actually want to say goodbye. What would happen after tonight? After Victor would fly back home? They'd wish each other the best of luck and remain vague Facebook friends?

She paused to think and caught a glimpse of herself in a window. A muted reflection of her large almond-shaped eyes looked back at her, above a nose dotted with just a few freckles. Freckles Victor referred to as "sweet cinnamon sprinkles." With a sigh, she supposed watching Godzilla on repeat wasn't such a bad thing. Funny how she hated the flick, herself. Maybe it was the half-Asian side of her rebelling. Her eyes traced to the tops of skyscrapers, imagining the giant ripping buildings apart like mere Legos in his lizard hands.

At the sight of smoke pluming out of a nearby apartment building, Victor's to be exact, Lacey shook her head, trying to expel her overactive imagination. But the smoke only increased. All at once, the flashing lights and unusual, static crowd made sense.

"Oh, no!" she gasped. Instinctively, she just ran.

She ducked under the police line tape, only to have her heel catch in a manhole lid, ripping it off. She nearly fell to her knees, but with fast reflexes she successfully kicked both shoes off and clung tight to her purse as she continued. Small bare feet slapped the wet sidewalk, her long black hair slashing back and forth.

Suddenly remembering apartments have sprinklers, she slowed her pace, letting the thought alleviate some of her anxiety. Victor would be okay. *He's safe*, she told herself. *Victor would have gotten out anyway.* Still, there was a darkness that tried creeping into her chest, as she neared the emergency personnel.

She asked the first person she came across, a tall woman in a robe, zombie-eyed in astonishment, "What caused the fire? Did someone leave an iron on? Was it a candle? What?"

The woman shrugged. "I don't know."

"Of course you don't know." Lacey bolted through the lobby door, not even hearing the officer calling out to her to stop. The fire crew had disabled the elevators, so she sped up the stairs, and raced down the hall toward his apartment, bursting through the small cluster of police officers still investigating the scene.

Victor's apartment was unrecognizable. The obscenely acrid scent nearly lifted her off her feet to throw her back out. Holding her nose, she stepped around the wet remains of charred boxes to the kitchen. Once-white countertops were black. Soot and ash littered the floor and climbed up the walls like a disease. She spotted a skillet teetered against skeletal remains of the cupboard space below the stovetop. Kneeling down, she stared at it, trying to gather her thoughts.

Glass shards poked out of a lump of soggy debris beside the skillet. Lacey lifted a large shard and rubbed the blackness off with her thumbs. There was a label to some cheap wine. That wasn't on par with Victor's taste.

Although he sometimes had cereal for dinner, wine was something he never skimped on… unless moving was making his wallet tighter than ever.

Setting the shard back down, she unsettled a bit of ash, exposing a small square something. Lacey plucked it out and wiped it off. A jewelry box? She lifted its lid.

"Victor?" she gasped at what was revealed. A brilliant diamond engagement ring flashed at her—a marquis cut, like she always wanted, on a platinum band.

Someone grabbed her elbow. She turned in surprise, successfully shoving the jewelry box into her long red blazer unseen.

The officer glanced at her bare feet and drenched hems to her slacks, saying, "We need this area clear." Although he spoke no English, Lacey understood.

She stood in shock, wiping back flyaway hairs. Out of habit, she reached for her press pass, but wasn't wearing one. "He was home? Cooking?"

"Yes." There was a solemn nod, then she was escorted out.

*

Victor threw himself to the ground and curled into the smallest possible ball. His attempts to envision Lacey were rebuffed, and his whole world shrank to a small cluster of emotions so vivid he could taste them. Despair, torment, envy, hatred! His vision imploded into a collapsing tunnel of hazy obscurity while tormented shrieks drowned out his hearing. The cold was now beyond description; the things were now sliding over his skin and penetrating his being.

"Please! Please… please…" Then his voice was gone.

LEGION! The word carried a terrifyingly triumphant note. At once, Victor realized, there were things worse than death. And he was experiencing one of those things first hand.

Then it was gone. All the pain and rending fear vanished like water under an atom bomb. Even though it was nighttime in Tokyo, everything was wrapped in brilliance. His vision, once darkened, had been miraculously enhanced. At a glance, he was able to make out the pores in the skin of a person looking out the window of an airliner passing overhead. The shrill cries of the damned had been replaced by a warm melody that was at once music, a fragrance and a sweet taste. Victor had no idea how that was possible, but he didn't care. He had been *saved*, and that was the only thing that mattered. Well, that and finding Lacey.

Leaping to his feet, Victor examined himself. He found it odd he was still wearing the same button-down shirt, tie, and slacks he'd been wearing when he came home from work. The clothing bore none of the marks of the attack, and he wondered how that was possible.

You really are *a newbie, aren't you?*

Victor looked around to see where the thought had come from. There was no one. "Hello? Hello? You're not another one of those freaky smoke devil things, are you?" His eyes scanned a full three-sixty, but found nothing.

You need to look higher, sweetheart, the thoughts said with oddly sarcastic patience.

He looked up. In the midst of the glowing scene one small, particularly bright light shone.

"You?" Victor asked. "What are you? You saved me, didn't you?"

He felt a sigh. *Do you really have to use your mouth?* the thing said. *You're dead. Don't expect me to flap my gums, even if you do.*

"Are you an angel?"

Another sigh. *Of course. Am I seriously going to have to teach you* everything *about being home again? They must have really worked you over when they plugged you into that mortal frame. Then again, your death was rather traumatic… Normally, people remember things much faster once they get back.*

19

Victor's brow scrunched. "What are you talking about? Get back from where?"

The light undulated slightly, and drifted down to his eye level. As it neared, it resolved itself into a shape he found he was startled to recognize.

"Ms. Tibbits?" He scoffed at the sight of his childhood cat.

The cat fairly glared at him. *It's "Rao," honey. It was you and those other humans that gave me that stupid name. "Ms. Tibbits." Pah. Anyway, you're safe. It looks like we're going to need a long talk. It's concerning that you didn't even remember the Dark Ones.*

He shuddered involuntarily. "Who—*what* were those—*things*?"

The black and gold tabby raised her eyebrow, completely surprising Victor.

What, Rao said. *Because only humans can have facial expressions and intelligent thoughts?*

"I, no, I mean… I just—"

She sighed again. *It's alright, kid. I'm just a tad frustrated by you waking up ignorant and defenseless. It's not terribly common. Don't let my tartness scare you. I guess being unable to talk to you humans for those seven years just really got on my nerves, you know? We cats are, well, more intelligent than you people think.*

"You mean, you wanted to talk to us before?"

She nodded. *Of course. You humans might not be the brightest creatures, when you're mortal, but you've got one grand lineage behind you. Once you're out of your faulty mortal frames, you're actually quite good company, for the most part.*

"Thanks," he said. "I think. But I still don't know what just happened, just then."

Come with me, deary. We'll take this slow, for your sake.

Victor watched as Ms. Tibbits—

Rao, thank you…

—didn't bother to jump down to the ground as he'd expected. Instead, she floated along, five feet off the ground, drifting rapidly ahead of him.

"How are you doing that?"

What? Moving without wagging my legs?

"Well, yeah." He fell in beside her, still wondering how it was that his childhood cat was alive and talking to him, at which Ms. Tibbits—

Rao!

—rolled her little green eyes—

Don't make me sound cute, Vic. I'm done with the "cute" thing, okay?

—and turned and looked at him, still drifting.

Let me give it to you straight, hon. You're not tied up in a mortal frame anymore. You're not chained to those stupid rules. Walking: what a waste of effort! Gravity bends to the will, dear; we just forget how to do it when we're tossed into mortality. Oh, and all those other "rules" of physics? You can throw those out, too. They're meant for that sphere, not for Reality. The rules here are even stricter, but they're looser at the same time.

Victor frowned. "Stricter... but... looser? How is that possible?"

She gave him a look of hopeless frustration. *I'm just going to show you.*

The expected magical gesture Victor was waiting for never came. One second, he was just outside his old apartment building. The next, it was just... there. All of it. Sights, sounds, history, thoughts, music, science. Like an entire doctorate-level education crammed into five seconds. When it was over, Victor dropped to his knees, feeling as though he should be panting.

"What was *that*?" He wasn't sure he'd even be able to remember a hundredth of what he'd just experienced.

Rao smirked. *It's called the joys of being immortal.*

"Great," he muttered. "But I need to get back to life. Lacey should be here any minute—hey, do you have the time?" he asked, tapping his wrist.

Right, Rao said, rolling her eyes, *because cats and Rolexes are a total thing. And you're not going back to your mortal life. If you want to know what time it is, it's time for you to stay here.*

"Can't, sorry, kitty. New job starts soon. Taniguchi gave me a gig in his Seattle branch. They won't be happy if I miss the first day."

How are you so dense about this? Rao asked. *Look, I came here to welcome you home. Now are you going to let me take you, or am I going to have to drag you?*

Victor looked his former pet in the eyes. "Okay. Let me be serious for just a moment. The woman I love is coming here any minute. Burned steaks aside, she's going to figure out pretty quick that our dinner date is off. Now maybe she won't cry her eyes out about this, but I'd like to see her just one more time. To say goodbye, if nothing else. Further, don't you think it was at least a *little* weird what happened at my place? Me falling all over myself after *one* glass of funky-flavored wine…" He trailed off, a disturbing thought rising in his mind.

I know what you're thinking.

"And I'm thinking," Victor said, "that there was more than just fermented grape juice in that snifter."

Of course. There was also yeast, sugar, and some sparkling water.

"Were you this sarcastic as a cat?"

I'm still a cat, she replied. *And yes I was. But all you humans could hear were ear-blowing screeches and yowls. How humiliating.*

"But you're thinking what I'm thinking? That my wine was—"

Poisoned? Well… forgive an angel for saying it, but, duh.

Victor sighed, pleased he could still do that. "So who would want to poison me?"

Well, Rao said, feigning ignorance, *let's see…*

Instantly, Victor knew that she knew. "So why aren't you just—"

Telling you? Rao interrupted. *Because you're coming home, so it doesn't matter. You'll find out when you get there. Now, let's be off.*

"Wait—don't I get some sort of 'vengeance from the

grave'?"

No… The look in her eyes was a mix of, "Why would you?" and "Your I.Q. is dropping by the moment."

"But, what about justice? I mean, crazy poisoner guy loose in Tokyo. I'm innocent, and he still took me out. What if he's some psychotic serial killer randomly poisoning—"

Handsome, yet desperate, American guys who are pining for their exes?

"Will you quit interrupting me?"

Will you quit asking stupid questions and let me escort you home? We're supposed to be doing the Hukilau in Heaven right now, not slumming in downtown Tokyo.

"I'm trying to prevent a crime."

Wow, Rao said, snorting. *You're too honest to make a good liar. So quit. Let's go.*

"No."

Rao rolled her eyes again, and gave him a look that reminded Victor a little too much of his own mom when she'd asked him something for at least the tenth time without his obedience.

"I want to know why I died. Heaven's not going anywhere. And I've got to see Lacey again."

Rao lifted a paw and counted on her claws. *Irrelevant, not quite accurate, but good enough, and… no chance. I win.*

Victor turned and strode back toward his apartment. He had no idea how he'd learn the identity of his killer, but he was pretty sure he wasn't making his flight the next day, so time was now on his side. Given that he also had some nifty new tricks up his sleeve, he guessed he would be able to figure something out—including how to stop a potential murderer from striking again. Oh, and he'd also figure out some Patrick Swayze move to get in touch with Lacey.

Yeah, Rao said, *and he's* really *a ghost now. You don't see him here. He's upstairs making the women swoon still.*

Victor walked through the lobby door (though he

couldn't *quite* convince himself to keep his eyes open) and strode toward the elevators.

This is stupid, Rao said, still floating beside him. *You're untrained and ignorant. The Dark Ones nearly had you for a late night snack out there. If I hadn't come along—*

"Then what, Ms. Tibbits?"

The name is—

"It's my turn to interrupt," Victor said, spinning and jabbing a finger at his dead pet. "Look, I appreciate you having my back out there. But I'm not ready to be dead. I don't know how they do things in Heaven, but I'm not going to be coerced into Paradise against my will, okay? I've got important things to do *here*, and they're as much about helping others as they are about helping myself. So if you're not going to give me a hand, I'll just figure it out myself."

With that, he spun on a heel and plowed toward the elevator. Stabbing the up button with his finger, he growled as the digit passed clean through the plastic "up" arrow. "You've gotta be kidding me," he grumbled. Realizing the elevators had been disabled anyway, he whirled for the stairs, charging blindly through the door and into the stairwell. Before he could make the first step, though, Rao was there, barring his way.

"Move it, Tibbits."

She sighed deeply. *Look, I'll make you a deal. Let me* at least *walk you through some basic survival techniques, and then you can knock yourself out, okay?*

Victor paused. "You're going to help me?" he asked hesitantly.

Not per se, she replied looking everywhere but at him.

"What's that supposed to mean?"

It means that I already know the whole story behind your death, its significance, and everything else. But if you're going to refuse to come, then I'm not allowed to tell. And rules are rules, so don't even think about asking me to skirt them. Think of this as your "Welcome home" present.

"You mean," he asked narrowing his eyes, "I can talk to Lacey again?"

Rao pursed her lips, and looked torn. Eventually, she relented. *If you can figure it out on your own, yes. But even if you do, she has to be* listening. *And that's just the barest tip of the iceberg when it comes to the rules of Reality.*

"So… you're going to help me?"

When I was mortal, I stayed with you because you kept putting food in my bowl. Don't push your luck, Vic.

"Well, then," he replied, beaming, "let's get this show on the road."

FOUR

Haunting downtown Tokyo in stylish duds appealed to Victor, though he wasn't accustomed to not being able to smell anything. Rao floated alongside him, still there, drawling through the lesson she'd begun when she'd agreed to help him in the stairwell. After enticing him with a few cool, but useless tricks—like being able to change his wardrobe at a whim—she'd pulled a bait and switch, telling him there were simply too many things to teach him in the course of one earth night. She then tried baiting him back to Heaven with pretty promises of being able to climb the learning curve almost instantly.

"Nice try, cat," he told her. She sighed again, and trailed just behind him, obviously not trying *too* hard to keep up; he was sure she was engaged in some sort of sullen protest. Just for fun, he switched to a new outfit, then another one a moment later.

Right, she said to his mind. *Because my self-esteem is so low it needs to be evaluated by a self-propelled haberdashery. Now can we get back to the lesson?*

"Call it a new nervous tick," he muttered, wondering both how Lacey would deal with the news, and how long it would take to get used to having raindrops fall *through* him, and his feet not splashing in puddles.

Your feet shouldn't even be in *the puddles*, Rao said. *You need to quit trying to use your legs so much.*

"God gave me legs, and they work just fine," he said. Realizing he'd reached Lacey's place, he halted suddenly, and Rao ran into his back.

"Lose your cat-like reflexes when you died?"

Oh, you're a riot, Vic.

"I just realized something," he said. "And before you go reading my mind and telling me what I'm about to say, just… don't."

She stuck her tongue out.

"What kind of angel are you, anyway?" Victor asked, wrinkling his nose.

Apparently one who merits punishments from the Big Man.

"Anyway," Victor continued, "as I was about to say, I just realized something."

Rao smirked. *You mean that you're a clueless idi—*

"Your insults are so inspiring I'm going to stop them before you inspire me to death. Or… something. As I was saying, I just had a thought—why was I the target of a burglary in the first place? If anyone had cased my apartment, they'd have known that, aside from my laptop and briefcase, I don't have much of value."

Rao frowned. *I could give you every answer to this whole mess if you'd let me.*

"Yeah," he said, "and then I'd be stuck in Heaven, unable to do anything about it."

Heaven's a pretty nice place, the former pet said. *You do realize that people are literally dying to get there, yes?*

A beat passed. Then another.

Okay, Rao admitted reluctantly, *that one was a bit dry…*

"As I was trying to say," Victor said, glaring at the cat, "there are just too many things that are off about this. I mean, I had my accounting files, my clothing, my laptop, some old college books, toiletries, and some cheap souvenirs for Mom and Dad. I already did the research on this part of Tokyo before moving here, and I picked the lowest-crime area I could afford. So what about me makes me a target?"

Your charming personality and matchless intelligence?

"Whose angel *are* you, anyway?"

The Big Man's. And He's waiting for you. Still.

Victor waved it away. "Well, I've got unfinished business. Doesn't that give me some sort of right to haunt people until my soul is at rest?"

Rao shook her head. *You're really not going to let this go, are you?*

The deceased accountant smiled. "Of course not." A motion caught his eye, and he brightened—literally—to see Lacey striding down the sidewalk. "Lacey!" he called, but she carried on as though he were a ghost.

Oh, Vic, you're killing me here. Ha! Pun totally intended!

Victor rolled his eyes and hurried after Lacey. "Hello?" he said. "Lacey? Tell me you can hear me, babe." She, of course, gave no sign of recognition whatsoever. He got out in front of her, spread his arms wide, and stopped.

She passed clean through him, giving him a strange, rippling sensation. "Dude," he said, "that's *weird*."

You get used to it. Now go get her, Romeo.

Sighing, Victor followed after her. He could feel, more than hear, her thoughts, but they tumbled out in such a jumble that he found he couldn't keep up. Glancing in dismay at Rao, he gestured at the woman he loved. "Are all women's minds this much of a mess?"

The tabby just shook her head and muttered something about "male stupidity."

*

It was becoming one of the fastest, and yet one of the

longest, nights of Lacey's life. Knowing Nainai's health was unstable, she decided to muster all the courage she could to give her a quick call at midnight. That's when Nainai expected Lacey to enter quietly through the front door and eventually sprawl out on a cot beside her; she needed a good excuse not to.

"Hello, Grandmother," Lacey said with a strong tone, although she wiped a tear.

"Since when do you call me that?" the weak voice answered in disapproval.

Lacey clutched her purse tighter against her stomach as she sat alone at a bus stop. Buses discontinued their routes at midnight, as she was well aware. Rain was pouring now, streaming loudly down her bench's overhang. "I'm sorry, Nainai. I call you Nainai."

"That's better. Now, why aren't you home yet? Must have had a fun night with Victor?" Lacey could imagine the wink.

She bit her lip. "No, it, uh, wasn't that. I'm just suddenly very tired. I think I'm going to stay at the Mitsui Garden Ginza." She spoke of the hotel directly across from where she sat. Tall and gray, its many dark blue windows mourned with her.

"Well, get your rest, then. That's what I'm going to do," Nainai said. "And take your time tomorrow, saying goodbye to Victor before he flies home."

Those words sent a tingle down Lacey's spine, being a little too metaphorically accurate.

"I will." She thought of Heaven. If Victor's beliefs were true, he'd probably already be there, having a great reunion with family… and perhaps even his beloved Ms. Tibbits whom Victor had carried a picture of in his wallet.

Lacey couldn't suppress the bittersweet sensation to smile at that. In the old, bent picture, Ms. Tibbits posed with so much attitude that Lacey often joked the cat must have been a reincarnation of her grandfather.

"Goodnight, Nainai."

"Goodnight, baby girl."

Moments later, Lacey checked herself into the semi-ritzy hotel, dropping $300 without thought. Her bare feet earned a glare, but she didn't care. She took the elevator to the seventh floor, and soon dropped face first on a king-sized bed.

"Why?" she cried some more. "Why did you have to beat me home? What were you *thinking*? You were going to try impressing me with your cooking? You know you can't do that!" She wailed into her pillow before punching at it. "You stupid man! Stick to Lucky Charms!"

Victor stood by her bed, Rao perched on an end table. He was speechless watching her. This was a very private moment for Lacey, he knew. Although she was wailing about *his* stupidness, it was never intended to actually be seen by him. Especially now... as she was tearing into the pillow with her teeth, snarling, her rear in the air.

"Maybe I should come back tomorrow morning," Victor said, taking a step back.

No, Rao said, a curiously tender note in her mental voice. *Lacey's hurting, right now—you can even feel it.*

Victor's brow wrinkled. "I—"

Just stop and be quiet for a moment, you dolt. You've always wanted to know how women worked. Here's your chance.

Victor opened his mouth again, but immediately thought better of it. Turning his attention to his ex-girlfriend, he felt a tsunami of emotion crash over him almost like a physical force. At once he understood her pain, her confusion, her sense of lost opportunities, her guilt as though maybe, somehow, possibly, she might have been the cause of his demise. He felt the grief of Lacey for her ailing grandmother, and the worry she had about whether her boss, Greg was *actually* coming on to her at work. The litany went on until Victor felt he should be gasping for breath. He forced his mind closed with a *snap*, and wheeled on his pet cat.

Careful what you wish for, she said, even as he brought up an accusing finger.

"You could have at least warned me."

Rao only smirked.

Victor chewed his lower lip, and turned his eyes on Lacey again.

"You weren't right for me, Victor," she was saying. Being dead allowed him to hear the words perfectly no matter how badly muffled by her pillow. "And you had to go and buy me a *ring*? What were you thinking? We were supposed to just fly home, and stay friends. Why did you have to go and *die*? You *idiot*."

Victor gave in to instinct, and knelt on the bed beside her. "Hey, Lace," he said, burying his face in her hair, and taking care not to accidentally push his nose through her scalp, "it's okay. I'm still here." He wrapped his arms around her, wishing he could hold her tight, just like he had once upon a time, and as he'd hoped to again, before that unidentified idiot had broken into his apartment. Even as Lacey mourned for the loss of Victor, Victor mourned for her losses, and the loss of what might have been. All at once the memories came, and to Victor he seemed to be living it all over again.

FIVE

Five months earlier...

Victor had always loved a good party. He hoped the ones in Tokyo would be as good as this one. He'd be there in only a few days, in his new internship, and Akio Taniguchi himself had traveled from Japan to host this bash for all the interns his company had selected for that summer. Victor had shown up at the designated hotel right on time.

He thought of Jessica, his ex-girlfriend. Had they not broken up, she would've been his "plus one." At first, she seemed like a goddess, magically missed by the rest of his graduating class. She was as stunningly single as she was beautiful. It hadn't, in the end, taken him long to figure out why she couldn't keep a man on her leash.

He pushed the blond leech out of his mind, and turned his thoughts to the present. Plenty of people, just like all the parties he'd been to before. He felt right at home in his dress shirt and slacks—no tie, thanks—and tried not to pay attention to certain "business" deals going on in some of the more shadowed corners. The openness with which certain… substances… passed around was something he still wasn't used to even after college; he'd never been that kind of guy, what with his Christian upbringing and all.

Whistling like he hadn't seen anything, he scanned the party again, breathing in the ambience that was corporate nightlife, and wondering how different Tokyo may be. Would there be this many attractive girls there? Most of them were just eye candy, though, a far cry from campus life at the University of Washington, with its more… self-possessed girls. Victor wasn't interested in fluff. He wanted *the* girl. Someone smart, maybe a bit sassy, and who knew who she was and where she was going. A girl who—

A hand clapped him on the shoulder. "Kombanawa, St. John-san. Are we enjoying the evening?"

Victor turned to see a statuesque Asian man in a suit that would have set Victor back probably a semester's-worth of tuition. Hints of silver streaked through his jet black hair along his temples, and the beginnings of lines around penetrating eyes. He was flanked by another Asian man, shorter, and almost wiry, with nervous eyes. An entourage trailed in his wake, composed of other interns and, of course, beautiful girls; Victor concealed a laugh at the way his fellow interns pandered for the man's attention.

Victor immediately doubled into a deep bow. "Kombanawa, Taniguchi-sama," he replied. "Thank you for inviting me to this party. It's an honor to be here, sir."

The Japanese businessman chuckled lightly, then in flawless English replied, "Please, Victor-san. You may address me as Taniguchi-senpai. I am your teacher, hai?"

"Hai, sir," Victor said, inwardly amazed at how this man was able to dispel his usual, carefree self by his mere presence. Then again, Taniguchi was *amazingly* well connected, and the fact that Victor was even *allowed* into his office as a junior accountant would open probably as many doors as his degree would. This internship was one he couldn't lose at any cost.

Mister Taniguchi grinned warmly. "You Americans. You take our ancient sense of honor too seriously; or not seriously enough, perhaps." The man cast a quick glance at the interns crowded behind him. Several cowered until he looked away. "But I like you, Victor-san. You are… an honest young man."

Victor tried not to let his swelling head become too obvious. "Arigatou, Taniguchi-senpai."

"I see you are practicing Japanese ahead of your time in my country. Impressive."

"Arigatou, sir."

Taniguchi waved the comment away. "Victor, I would like you to meet one of my many associates. Allow me to introduce Orochi Watanabe, Chief Financial Officer of our partner firm, Mizuko Accounting."

Victor bowed deeply again. Watanabe refused to return his bow, Victor began to wonder. The look in the other man's eyes was anything but welcoming.

"Do not mind Orochi," Taniguchi said with a small laugh. "He treats everyone like this. Even, once the emperor himself."

Watanabe's eyes tightened, and he threw a sidelong glance at his colleague, which was quietly but pointedly ignored. "I believe," the older man continued lightly, "Orochi may be able to give you some valuable advice, during your stay in our country. He is a most skilled accountant, and understands international commerce exceedingly well."

Victor inclined his head at the other man, and kept his clenched fists discreetly behind his back. Watanabe grunted but, at a look from Taniguchi, managed to nod almost politely. And just like that, Victor's boss surged off into the crowd, which parted around Victor, leaving him too breathless and stunned to notice his fellows giving him the same, cold looks that Jessica had given him when he'd read her his acceptance letter to Kyoto Consulting.

He sighed, and made his way over to the bar. To the bartender's surprise, he ordered root beer (why did everyone look at him funny when he did that?) He wanted to enjoy tonight *and* remember it. All around him swayed people who provided ample support for his reasoning. He thought about a couple glasses of white wine, just for the taste, but he was still in America, so he figured he'd get an all-American drink, just in case he couldn't find any in Japan.

The bartender handed him his drink and Victor reclined against the bar to resume his search, wondering at the people who had come. These were intelligent people. People with clout and savvy. People with *power*, who could make things happen. So why would he rather be kayaking the Puget Sound instead of schmoozing and trying to get ahead?

He stood, suddenly wondering where the nearest exit was. Spotting it, he fast-walked over, pushing it open with a shoulder. He emerged into where cool air and solitude greeted him. He wiped his brow in relief, and glanced down the hotel's hallway, just to see what else was going on that evening.

Next door's banquet room had a door ajar. He meandered past, taking a curious look inside. Under dim lights, throbbing music kept the partygoers dancing—including some clearly drunk guy moving as though he were climbing an invisible wall—while others mingled near strategically-located tables laden with hors d'oeuvres. The people in there were dressed... *richer*, if that were possible, than the ones at Taniguchi's shindig.

He stepped closer, peeking carefully in. There were quite a few beautiful women. It was interesting how everyone had perfectly coiffed hair, some looking like live Barbie and Ken dolls. Their smiles were practiced. The way they greeted each other with air kisses and hearty handshakes also felt superficial. However, there was one woman in the distance who wasn't like the rest…

The Asian woman wore her long and loose black tendrils well, framing a pretty face. She was more real. She had an air of class above the rest. The way she crossed her slender legs, clutched her purse, wore a simple tennis bracelet with her black cocktail dress. He could stare at her for… forever.

A bellboy rolling a rack of tuxedos interrupted his thoughts. "Can I help you, sir? Are you lost?"

Victor stepped back from the door as if being caught doing something against the law. "Me? No."

The bellboy looked to be maybe eighteen years old, a fresh zit on his forehead. "Is there something I could help you find?" he asked.

Victor opened his mouth in thought. "Well, come to think of it, I am actually lost. I was at the party next door, in that hall"—he pointed—"but I believe I'm supposed to be in here, in this hall." He meant every word of that, thinking of the mystery woman.

The bellboy smiled. "We don't have bouncers at the door. You can just go in, sir."

Victor pulled out his wallet in thought. Should he ask? "Listen, um…" He rifled through a few dollar bills and a five. He definitely was on a tight budget. Being a student did that to ya. "What would it take to borrow one of these fine tuxedos you have there? I don't have much, but…"

The kid smiled big. He had braces, even. "I'll do you a favor. Tell me your size." Victor did, and the kid rifled through the rack for a few moments before producing a pair of slacks and a coat for Victor's consideration. "These belong to the hotel. They're for 'just in case,' so I don't think my boss will mind me letting you borrow one. There's a restroom, right over there, around the corner. Just return it to me by twelve midnight. No tip necessary."

Victor's blue eyes widened. "Well hot dang. A hotel that keeps tuxedos on hand for random guys like me. I guess fairytales do come true…"

*

"Who is that guy?" Lacey asked Cathy Higgins, her editor and friend. "Is he new?"

Cathy put her cat-eye glasses to the very tip of her nose in drunken thought. "Phil, our janitor?"

Phil was in the center of the dance floor, busting a move like washing tall windows, his belly jiggling along. A circle of people crowded around him, clapping, looking all the more foolish for being so stylishly dressed.

"Noooo." Lacey shook her head. She shifted her position on the hotel's stylish leather couch. "That guy!" She pointed to a handsome man standing in the doorway, people-watching under dark eyebrows.

Cathy perked up, and fixed her short red hair. "I don't know, but I call dibbs!"

"We're not fourteen, Cathy! You don't call dibbs."

"Well, the whole online dating thing lately has run dry, after my last three psycho dates. Let's not forget the cable guy. So I think I have the right to call," and she hiccupped, "dibbs."

The guy glanced over. Lacey felt her heart skip. He did a double-take, fixing his gaze on her. He smiled. She couldn't help but smile back.

Turning back to Cathy, Lacey was expecting to get a scolding, but instead found her friend passed out with a snore. Satisfied, she turned her gaze back to the stranger, but instead found network producer, and co-owner of channel KZTB, Greg Mendoza suddenly before her. Her boss wasn't too shabby to look at—wavy black hair, tan skin—but he was married… and a little eccentric.

"Lovely Lace," he said, holding a martini. "How goes it this evening?"

"Great!" Lacey said, standing up to meet him at eye

level. She instinctively pulled the hem of her tight black dress down to her knees. "I'm enjoying what you've put together here."

"It's amazing, right?" He extended an arm toward the party scene. A disco ball glittered down from the tall hotel banquet room, sending zigzagging neon lights across what could easily be over a hundred guests. In the distance, a banner filled nearly half the wall, celebrating thirty years of KZTB's morning news program, *Good Day Seattle.*

"Yes, yes." Lacey nodded, an irrational nervousness making her toes curl just a bit in her pointy-toed heels. That was painful. "You really knocked it out of the park, boss."

Greg set his free hand on her shoulder, his brown eyes looking intently into hers. "Tonight, don't call me boss, okay? I'm just a friend having a good time."

"Where's your wife?" The question sprang from her mouth without thought.

"My wife?" He paused. "She's, uh, you know, not feeling too well. Her headaches. Bad headaches."

Lacey glanced past Greg to the doorway. Dark Eyebrows guy was gone. There was no sign of him in the dimly-lit hallway beyond, either, nor could she pick him out in the crowded room. She grimaced. *Shoot!*

Greg cut in. "I was thinking, Lacey. Let's say we get back to business Monday, at a lunch meeting. I've been mulling over some opportunities. I know how you've been eyeing the lead anchorwoman position."

That got her attention. "Yes? Deborah's not leaving, is she?" Deborah had been lead anchorwoman for seventeen-point-five years now. Perky. Pretty. Perky. Rumors flew that Kelly Rippa herself was envious of the brunette star. Lacey glanced around and noticed Deborah at the bar. The woman looked away suddenly as if she'd been caught staring.

"No, no, no." He shook his head with a wide Cheshire cat smile across his tan face. "Deborah is staying. There's another opportunity that's presented itself that I think would be perfect for you, however, if you'd be in. It could make you nationally, no, *internationally* known. I'll leave it at that." He patted her shoulder, chewed the olive out of his martini glass and sauntered away.

"Well," Lacey said out loud in curiosity.

"He seems interesting," a man said playfully, a hint of sarcasm peeking through.

Lacey looked over her left shoulder, confirming what she thought. It was *the* guy. "Oh," she simply said, turning to him.

"Lacey Ling, right?" he asked, extending a hand.

"I'm sorry, have we met before?" she asked, shaking it.

"So to speak. TV. Yeah, you probably get that all the time, but you're…" he paused, and she could tell he was weighing his words, "…you're hard to miss. You did a live report at the U of W, not long ago. I was actually in the background for that one."

"Oh, of course. Your name would be…?"

"St. John—Victor St. John," he said with a wry smile, speaking like he was Bond. He had pretty white teeth, like the character. He then ran a hand through his dark hair that bounced perfectly back into place. Lacey wondered how much Palmade he used. Regardless, it looked good.

"I'm teasing." He chuckled.

She let herself laugh. "Of course. So… what is your position with the program? I don't believe I've seen you on set. Or in the production room."

"That's because I don't work for KZTB." He shrugged, and she couldn't help but notice how well his tux fit him. It didn't hurt that his dress shoes had a mirror polish that went well with his gold cuff links, and slick bowtie.

This guy's probably super conceited, probably has a girlfriend or two… Which took her to her next thought. "I get it—you're a guest of someone. Karina?" Lacey glanced over at the bombshell chatting it up with other girls.

"No, I came alone." The sparkle in his blue eyes showed he liked the anticipation of playing the 'mystery man' game.

Lacey posted a hand on her hips and cocked her head. "Do I need to ask twenty questions to find out just what you're doing here?" It was her turn to smile. Okay, so she could go for a good game, occasionally.

"Yes, twenty questions."

She bit her lip, thinking. "Question number one—how much hairspray do you use?"

"Hey now, what's that got to do with—"

"Doesn't matter. I get to ask whatever I wish."

"But they also have to lead to yes or no answers."

"Do you always play by the rules?" She arched a brow.

He tugged at his bowtie. "Me? Hardly. So the answer is 'no.' That's two questions down, Miss Ling."

Eighteen questions, and two hours later, the two believed in love at first sight.

SIX

Four months earlier…

Victor had never had a better month in memory. Though his Japanese was only just adequate, he still greeted the perky receptionist on his way into the main lobby of Kyoto Consulting and smelled *business*; and business was good. That optimism was reflected in the polished marble flooring, the confident looks on the faces of other employees, all of whom wore the uniforms of the corporate elite, and even in the really cool waterfall that cascaded down from the second floor on the far side of the lobby.

Victor vowed he would play in that waterfall at least once before leaving Japan.

He strode to the elevator, chin held high, and barely managing to contain his smirk. It had taken him the better part of his first week at Kyoto Consulting to stop trying to say hello to everyone, regardless of whether they were engrossed in a phone or a tablet. His mentor had set him straight on protocol fairly quickly, which Victor would later learn had saved him just enough face to avoid an early termination.

Four grueling weeks of being a glorified courier and coffee runner had done nothing to get Victor down. By the time the summer was up, Victor was sure Mister Taniguchi would be making him an offer; and a good one. Hopefully in the Seattle branch, but he was learning to love Tokyo, even if he hadn't seen his apartment in three straight days.

It's like Navy SEAL training, he kept telling himself. *They're just playing mind games. Weeding out the slackers from the rest of us.* And so it was that he set out to make this day the best day he'd had yet; and the best was yet to come. Lacey was set to arrive in Tokyo later today, and was on assignment here for *two weeks*. The thought brought a smile to his face as the elevator doors closed, hiding the scowls of at least two other Kyoto Consulting employees who probably thought he was smiling at their misfortune of missing the elevator by mere seconds. Victor was too caught up in the vision of Lacey to care.

He managed to make it to his desk after only two tries, but found that focusing on work was harder than he thought. Instead of tracking quarterly profit margins and figuring out how he was going to cart five cups of coffee to as many co-workers, he found himself checking and rechecking directions to Tokyo International Airport. His distraction nearly caused him to dump a cup of steaming coffee on a fellow employee, but he saved it in time, and managed to bow his way out of the man's heated rebuke (almost none of which he understood, though the man's tone needed no translation). Forcing himself back on task, he prevented himself from screwing up deliveries. Remembering that he was doing this *for* Lacey propelled him forward to lunch.

Lunch was the typical affair—lock his computer, instead of logging off, grab his pre-made meal, and head to the little garden area Kyoto Consulting had built into the center of its main office building. A quaint affair, the garden had real grass, fed by a small stream. The location of the garden blocked enough of the ambient smog that Victor could actually smell the cherry blossoms on the two trees standing in the middle of it all. Two or three others were seated on benches, glued to their tablets as they sucked protein shakes through straws. They'd never bothered Victor, and he'd given up trying to talk to them, though he was sure they were nice people. Taking his seat under one of the trees, he glanced at his phone to check the time, even as he hastily bit into his sandwich.

When he leaned back against the tree, something dug into his back. Turning, he was surprised to see a small box wrapped in plain, brown paper and tied with cheap string.

"Hello," he said, noticing a note under the string. "What brings you to the garden today?" He bent down to peer at the note. To his surprise, it was written in several languages, including English.

"He who gives anonymously," he read softly, "is more blessed than he who parades his gift." Victor raised his eyebrows. "Sounds a little too 'New Testament' for Japan, but hey, Buddhism has some pretty cool sayings too." He read on.

"Please, if you find me, open me." With a shrug, he did as the message said.

And his jaw dropped.

Inside, placed just above pictures of Japanese children clearly hard on their luck was a carefully folded wad of cash. Victor felt his face flush, and he looked around, wondering whether someone would take him for a thief. A note inside caught his eye. He slipped it out, while quietly turning and sitting on the box and its mother lode, and read the note. It was simple—the children pictured had been identified as being "in need." The note included information for an anonymous charity account that had been set up for such children, and instructed anyone who found the money to please deposit it, and to show the teller the pictures of the children involved. The bank in question had agreed to match the anonymous donation yen for yen in helping the kids.

And Victor was the man who got to make the deposit.

He frowned. "How'm I going to get to the bank before it closes?" The Japanese had a very different idea of "business hours" than he was accustomed to, and while he was certain the banks probably stayed open later as well, he didn't think they'd be open late enough to accommodate his schedule.

Then it hit him—he was an accountant, and he was a courier. Surely he could figure out *some* reason to get Mister Nagamo to let him make a trip. At once, he felt a plan begin congealing in his mind.

*

Victor's plan worked. In the name of "market research," he'd persuaded his supervisor to allow him to visit several local banks to discuss accounting practices with them. Nagamo had been skeptical, citing the fact that Kyoto Consulting had well-established guidelines, and that it already followed market practices to the letter. He argued that Victor was just trying to be a sight-seeing tourist, and that he was lazy. That changed when Victor suggested that he might be able to grab some American coffee from a specialty shop along his route, and that a free cup of the stuff might just make its way on to his boss's desk before the afternoon was out.

Who'd have thought the man would have been so easy to buy?

Even as he walked into the bank designated by the note, he found he was still shaking his head at the hungry look in his mentor's eyes, especially when he'd promised extra caramel sauce and whipped cream. Victor smiled as he queued up for the teller, and let his thoughts drift back to Lacey while he waited.

He'd been more than a little skeptical at first. Coming off his bleeding retreat from Jessica, he vowed he wasn't going to find someone on the rebound. Then, the night of Taniguchi's party had come, and the rest was history. He kept telling himself to put the brakes on—that this was all just some hormonal-adrenal response—but Lacey was just too good for him to convince himself it wasn't right. Her wit, her intelligence, those knowing eyes; she had everything he'd wished for in Jessica, but had only *thought* he'd found.

One thing led to another, and by the time he was on the plane to Tokyo, he was starting to wonder whether wedding bells may be in their future.

"Hello, sir?" The lilting voice broke his reverie, and he found himself standing at the front of the line. Blushing slightly, he cleared his throat and stepped forward, placing the pictures of the children on the counter, along with the note. Behind thick glass, a Japanese girl in a navy blue bank uniform smiled at him, a query in her eyes.

"I'm to deposit this money," he said, carefully laying the stack of yen notes next to his other pile, "into the account listed here. The money is for the children listed on the paper."

The teller looked at Victor's offering, then shot a strange glance at him. "Do you also wish to remain anonymous, sir?"

Victor smiled. "He who gives anonymously is more blessed than he who parades his gift, right?"

The teller straightened and blinked, suddenly seeming to come alive. "Of course, sir. An old proverb. Thank you for your deposit. May I assist you in some other way?"

Victor shook his head. "That'll be all, thanks." The teller bowed slightly, and Victor returned the bow, unable to keep from smiling, picturing the faces of the kids as they got new clothing, or, maybe, were moved into a new apartment or something. It felt wonderful. So wonderful, in fact, that he decided to head straight to the coffee shop and get his boss a double. Yes, today was a very good day.

A text message dinged. He pulled his phone out of his pants pocket to view it: *Hey, handsome. I was just thinking about you, again. Why'd we ever break up? Kissies & squeezies, Jessica.*

Well, it *had been* a good day—past tense. He'd ignore that text, along with the others piling up as of late. He knew she only liked "the chase." Anyway, it was a little nutty for a girl as gorgeous as her to keep pushing for a reply. Maybe he'd eventually block her number, and be done with it for good. And with that thought, he swiped his touchscreen and did block her.

As quick as that, Victor was back to having a very good day.

SEVEN

The memory of Jessica kicked Victor out of his reminiscence. *Ugh*, he thought. *So glad I got away from her. I thought she was going to be the death of me. Shrink wrap wouldn't have clung on to me as tightly as she did.*

He turned back to where Lacey was still sobbing on the bed. He'd unconsciously fallen prone next to her, his arm still draped across her shoulders. When her tears subsided some, she sat up, and he mirrored her. For the first time since getting here, he took a moment to take in his surroundings.

Lacey had really gone all-out picking a hotel. A king bed serviced by twin glass nightstands made a comfortable centerpiece for the room. The white wood dresser matched a desk sporting a large screen computer, and contrasted with the dark wood paneling covering the wall behind the bed. Another wall—this one all glass—opened on to a breathtaking view of the city, the famous Tokyo tower a swooping, red finger in the neon night.

"She must have really wanted a night out," he muttered.

Rao floated down and curled up on the bed, just the way she did when she was alive. She licked herself casually, and cast her eyes toward Victor. *Why do you do that?*

"What?" he asked.

Mutter under your breath.

"Why did you used to make those weird moaning sounds every spring evening?"

Rao looked as offended as a cat possibly could and, though she couldn't blush, Victor felt a wave of embarrassment ripple forth from her. *I'll thank you very much not to pursue that line of questioning.*

"And I'll thank you," Victor replied with a smile, "to not try psychoanalyzing every little thing I do. I'm here to help Lacey. You said I could talk to her if I could figure out how, so I need to start somewhere. For all I know, she'll still be on a plane soon, and she'll leave any clues behind that might point to my killer. And besides…" he trailed off, looking at the Asian beauty wistfully.

Rao's paw brushed against his hand. *I know how you feel about her, Victor,* the cat said with surprising tenderness. *Believe it or not I was in love once. With five different toms, but… it's a cat thing. You're a good guy, Vic, even if you're an idiot. She'd have done well to get you.*

Victor nodded, but kept his thoughts on Lacey. He could still sense her tangle of thoughts, and wondered whether he could unravel them, the way he used to unravel his grandma's yarn balls.

Grandma always hated that, Rao mused cheerily. *I loved it, of course. Oh, and thanks for taking the hit every time she caught you entertaining me.*

"You're welcome," Victor murmured, trying to fixate on just *one* of his girlfriend's thoughts. Once again, they seemed to go in a million different directions at once. She never seemed to think of any one thing for more than a few seconds before she moved on to something that seemed to have little-to-nothing to do with the previous thought. After only a minute, his head hurt; he wasn't aware that was even possible.

"I give up," he said, extricating himself from the mental mess. And yet, he couldn't quite shut it out.

I could teach you how to—

"We've been through that, too, yes," Victor interrupted. "I just don't like your price."

Rao rolled on to her back, paws in the air, and Victor absently reached out to scratch her underbelly. *There are other ways of reading thoughts, you know. And you should also know that you're handling it like a guy. No wonder you're not getting anywhere with it.*

Lacey stood up, and walked into the bathroom, where she turned on the sink's faucet, and splashed some water on her face. Victor watched as she peered at her reflection, and found himself doing the same. He couldn't get over just how beautiful she was. "Care to enlighten me, oh wise Cat of Heaven," he said quietly, still intent on the sadness in Lacey's eyes.

Well, think of it like merging on to a freeway.

Victor screwed up his face. "How would *you* know what that's like?"

Rao put on a big, happy cat smirk. *First-hand experience. I found out what happens when you try it on foot. And you just thought I'd run away.*

Victor felt himself go cold, and knew that if he'd still had a heart in his chest, it would have paused. "Oh my gosh," he whispered, whirling to face the tabby. "You… you…"

Met a tire at sixty-five miles per hour, give or take. But that's okay. It didn't hurt, and all my kittens were grown. But focus. Look at Lacey.

He complied.

Now, don't focus on anything except gauging the speed and flow of her thoughts.

"How am I supposed to—?"

You don't think about it, for starters. You just do it. Find an opening, and merge on into the traffic flow.

Victor tuned into her thoughts and was, once again, almost immediately swept away. After a few moments, he caught on to another thought about Lucky Charms, which evolved into how Lacey hated the way Victor ate, which morphed into a reminder that she hadn't eaten since lunch. The thoughts continued to blur and flash, all punctuated by various emotions, but Victor closed his eyes, and let himself drown in it all. At once, he realized that he *wasn't* completely lost anymore. Though the way forward was anything but linear, he found he was finally able to swim with the tide, and get a general sense of where she was going. It was as though he were standing in a giant, domed room with a billion different movies playing across the ceiling all at once, with literal surround sound. He was pleasantly surprised when he sensed dubiousness and suspicion regarding his death.

"Yes—yes!" he called to her mind. "Run with that. Help me out, Lace."

His thoughts faltered for a moment, and many of the images were replaced with pictures of Victor, along with thoughts of how handsome, confident, and utterly stupid he was. It was simultaneously flattering and insulting.

"Can you hear, Lacey? Hello?"

Lacey peered into the mirror, frowning. She squeezed her eyes shut, and shook her head lightly before splashing more water on her face.

Not bad, Vic. Maybe you're remembering more than I gave you credit for. The cat patted his shoulder. *Now, I'll give you a teensy, tiny hint. You can stroll through* her *memories, too.*

Victor blinked out of Lacey's mind, and frowned. "And why would I want to do that?"

Well, Rao drawled, prowling around in the air at eye level, *you might just find something that helps you… understand why you're here. Or, as you prefer to think, "dead."*

Victor squinted. "I thought you said, on the way here, that you were bound by an oath not to reveal certain secrets before I returned to Heaven."

Rao actually whistled innocently.

Victor glared at his pet. "There's a caveat, isn't there?"

Nope. And no, I'm not breaking any rules. You still need to know what to look for, and how to get there in the first place. Might as well get started.

Lacey moved back into the bedroom, and touched the desk phone. Victor practiced merging into her thoughts—it was a little easier this time—and found she was contemplating ordering room service.

"Ask for Lucky Charms," he said, noticing that a few images of leprechauns appeared across the screen of her mind. Lacey chewed her lip, and picked up the phone, then put it down again and sank back into the bed.

Try it, Rao said. *She's got some really fun stories to see.*

Victor bit his lip. "That seems a bit… violating, don't you think?"

Rao sighed and rolled her eyes. *Look, outside mortality, thoughts aren't hidden. We all share. Yes, it's a bit bothersome and embarrassing once you've been locked in a mortal frame for a while, but you get used to it. Really, I'm doing you a favor.*

"Some favor," he muttered.

Really—try it, she repeated.

"Where do I even start?" Victor asked, sitting next to Lacey, and reaching out to stroke her head. He smiled when she absently placed a hand over the area he was stroking.

How about, Rao said pensively, *the first time she came to visit you here.*

Victor raised an eyebrow. "And I'm looking for what, exactly?"

Ah, ah! Secrets.

"Whatever. Okay. Onward and upward. Or something." With that, he slipped back into Lacey's mind and began his search, even while she drifted off to sleep. With her mind wavering, he found that reading her was less like freeway traffic, and more like swimming in a massive school of fish. And with a few hours of fishing, he managed to find what he was looking for before sunrise.

For the first time in memory, he understood what it was like to be a woman. He also finally figured out just why Lacey hated flying.

EIGHT

Two months earlier…

Lacey's insides were dancing. The airplane's seatbelt seemed to chafe at her shifting, so she loosened it just a touch, then straightened her hair. The stale air from the vent over her head seemed to be aimed more at annoying her than at keeping her cool, so she twisted the nozzle closed, before digging in her purse for a piece of gum. She glanced behind her to check on the camera crew. The two men seemed to be doing fine.

"Nervous about flying?"

Lacey glanced up and across the aisle to where Greg Mendoza was smiling at her. "I used to get that way. Learned long ago that all you need is the right distraction."

Lacey faked a smile in return. "Thanks, boss. And again, thank you so much for taking me along on this."

Greg waved it away. "Hey, no worries. We're family at KZTB. Besides, I still remember my first time flying. Thought I was going to be sick." He chuckled lightly. "Sorry, that probably wasn't very helpful."

The overhead PA chimed. Lacey gave her boss another

polite smile, and turned her attention to the announcement. She wouldn't mention to the man that her nerves had nothing to do with flying—something she was totally fine with—and *everything* to do with seeing Victor again.

"Ladies and gentlemen, this is your captain speaking. I, ah, know we're running a little behind." Half the passengers, most of them certainly heading to Tokyo on business, groaned.

"And," he added, "we are just a bit overbooked. As such, we are asking for three volunteers to take a later flight."

Lacey rested her head back. She wouldn't be one of the volunteers.

A bald man, his shiny scalp glinting in the overhead lights, called out, "I volunteer as tribute!" There were a few chuckles of relief.

Almost immediately after, Lacey spotted something else glinting—her boss's gold watch, as he shot his hand in the air.

Oh, no, she thought. *What's he thinking?*

"See you in Japan." Greg patted Lacey on the knee, giving her a "take care" kinda wink.

Outside was dark, since it was eight-oh-five p.m. Lacey really, *really* didn't want to make the night go any longer. She already dreaded possibly snoring in front of her coworkers. She sat up taller in her seat, looking behind her. The cameramen were squirming in their seats over whether or not one of them should go with the boss. Her business savvy quickly prodded her to do the only right thing under the circumstances.

"I'll go!" She raised her hand high.

Her boss smiled, peering at her with oddly satisfied eyes.

A flight attendant ushered the three volunteers to gather their carry-on bags and quickly exit.

Walking back down the long hall back into the airport, Lacey's boss said, "I was afraid I'd be stuck with one of the camera guys. They wouldn't be nearly as good company. Whaddya say we lounge in the airport's sushi bar for a bit? And don't worry, the night's on KZTB."

Lacey forced a smile. "Thank you. I guess I will."

*

The sushi bar was pretty empty. Only a couple other patrons sat, at separate small tables, lazily eating. *Their flights must have been delayed, and they have nothing better to do, too*, Lacey mused.

At the bar, Greg whipped open his folded napkin, and laid it gingerly across his beige slacks. He then loosened his shiny purple tie with a sigh. "I'm actually pretty hungry," he said. "I think I'll order a whole roll."

Lacey followed his example, laying her napkin neatly across her black pencil skirt. "I've got a pretty healthy appetite myself, tonight."

Since it was an airport "restaurant," the menu was pretty minimal. Lacey was happy to see her favorite sushi on the list—smoked salmon over rice. Before closing her menu, she spotted the Godzilla Roll, and thought of Victor. In honor of seeing him soon, she mentally switched her preference.

Upon her ordering, Greg chuckled. "I wouldn't have taken you for a fan of the Godzilla."

"Really?" she asked, curious. "What would you have guessed?"

He paused, evidently liking the challenge. "I see you as liking one of the classics. Hmmm, the smoked salmon."

"Good guess." She laughed.

"Then why didn't you order it?"

"Broadening my horizons?" She arched a brow.

"Oh, is that all then?"

Lacey pressed her full lips together, a bit uneasy. Somewhere in her moral compass, she considered it in poor taste to discuss private affairs with those in positions of authority, above her. The other part of her, which was excited about seeing Victor soon, didn't care—she wanted to blab about her boyfriend, even if it was to her boss.

"Well?" Greg prodded with a knowing smile, as if he were a mind reader. "I knew it. There's another reason, isn't there?"

"Okay, I'll tell you. I'm dating someone who is pretty much obsessed with Godzilla." She felt herself blush in embarrassment.

Greg gave an interested nod in response. "You mean he has, like, the action figures posed on shelving in his apartment. That kind of obsessed?"

"Well, not that I'm aware of. Maybe he hides those before I come over." She was serious. Suddenly, she wondered what that implied for their relationship. A guy who played with action figures? Who did that? But there was so much to love about him that she could ignore it.

"At least you know what to get him for Christmas, huh?" He nudged her. "Don't worry. He'll grow out of it… maybe."

"Hm," she simply said. In the moment, Greg didn't actually seem like such a bad guy.

The sushi was promptly served. Lacey used chopsticks while Greg opted for silverware. He dug into his Rainbow roll, layered with bright orange salmon, dipping it liberally in wasabi. Lacey very purposefully swished her fried roll into her soy sauce boat, no wasabi, as it was already burning her tongue right off the plate.

They chatted for over an hour. Greg ordered two cups of saké from the bartender. This allowed for him to open up about *his* personal affairs, namely with his wife. Turns out, Greg had been telling the truth about her headaches and the problems they caused. Lacey couldn't help but feel bad for him, and despite herself, she found herself offering solace.

Stop it, Lacey, she said, as the night wore on. *Stay out of his personal life.*

"So," Greg finally said, his speech slightly slurred, "tell me more about this monster-loving boyfriend of yours. I've done all the talking tonight."

Lacey smiled, demurring slightly. "Well," she said, "things happened kind of fast between me and Victor."

Greg raised his eyebrows.

"Not like that," she hastily added. "Just… well, it was at that party you threw three months back."

"Ah," he said. "I don't recall any 'Victor' working for our station. New guy? Did H.R. let in another intern without consulting me?" He smiled easily.

Lacey tucked a strand of hair behind her ear. "Actually," she said, blushing, "he crashed the party."

Greg's eyebrows went up again. "My kind of guy." He leaned forward and patted Lacey's knee twice. "Keep hold of him. Which station does he work for? Maybe we can steal him away."

Lacey glanced down the concourse, wishing they'd call her new flight. "He's an accountant, actually. Interning in Japan."

"Well," Greg said, leaning forward and folding his hands, "we can use another good accountant. And how very lucky for you that I tapped you for this trip. Great experience for you and a free trip to see Mister Right. When's the big day?"

Lacey's eyes widened and she waved her hands. It was all she could do to keep from sputtering. "Mister Mendoza, sir—"

"You need to quit calling me that. Mister Mendoza is my father. I'm Greg."

Lacey paused. "Right. I barely know the guy. I mean, he's charming, and intelligent, and handsome—come to think of it, he's actually gorgeous…" She trailed off, smiling to herself. Before she could resume, a woman's voice came over the PA announcing the flight.

Greg glanced at his watch. "Wow. Will you look at the time? Good thing I can sleep on a flight; I'm gonna need it after that saké."

"I hear saké is bad for your health," Lacey said, standing and collecting the few bags she brought with her.

"Nice that my employees care about me," Greg said, fishing some loose bills out of his wallet and dropping them on the table before standing not altogether steadily. "And Lacey," he said, stepping forward and placing his hand on her arm, "I do mean that. As the guy who has to answer for all the crew, it's nice to think they may be looking out for me too. That's what makes us a family. Thank you again for getting off the flight."

Lacey smiled, a small sense of pride blossoming inside. She'd made a good impression on the boss again. That may not mean much now, but she knew the value of small steps. Speaking of which, she'd have to have a little chat with Victor about considering making their own steps a little smaller when it came to their new romance. She couldn't deny that it had been almost *too* much fun, though. Still, she couldn't deny how she felt about him. She'd focus on work while in Japan, yes, but her off hours? She knew exactly with whom she'd be spending them.

*

Lacey's stay in Tokyo was entirely too focused on work. More precisely, her boss. Between that and Victor's own, insane schedule, she found that what was meant to be time getting to know her new man evaporated as soon as it appeared. Even the one day when the KZTB group made a surprise appearance at Kyoto Consulting, she'd barely gotten more than a glimpse of Victor. Of greater concern was that it was quickly becoming apparent that they'd need more than text messages and perfunctory phone calls if they wanted to turn a quick fling into something lasting.

The memory of one of their final conversations, shortly before she'd flown home, surfaced. They'd met in the lobby of his apartment; she'd resisted his invitations to come up, and when he'd appeared to greet her, her face was closed.

When they'd greeted, he kissed her, and held her tight. He gushed about how he'd spent his summer helping needy Japanese children through surprise and random acts of charity; something about finding "gifts" in various places, then depositing the money in banks around town. The situation instantly raised red flags with Lacey, but she still had business to do in Tokyo, and precious little time to do it.

"I don't have the time to visit further, Victor," she'd said, wondering how well her eyes could hide what she felt. "Greg—Mister Mendoza has me on a lead here."

"What kind of lead?" Victor asked eyes narrowing.

She looked away, and she could tell Victor would get the hint not to push it. She'd given him a quick wave and an even briefer kiss goodbye. She felt like a liar, and could sense his eyes on her all the way to the double doors of the lobby. She took a deep breath. She should tell him. Or, at least, give him something to cushion the blow. Pausing, she turned, and put on her most sympathetic face. "We'll talk more later," she said. "I have a deadline. And... a lot to think about."

She felt her heart sink at the tone of her own voice. She could tell she'd just announced a break up. Knowing Victor, he was probably already taking it hard. He hadn't been good at hiding the fact that he was playing for keeps, despite the rapid-fire pace of their relationship. He tried playing it off smoothly, as she turned again for the door, but she knew they both were well aware that what had started with a bang between them, was just about to end with a fizzle.

NINE

Present Day…

The memories faded with the shake of his head, and Victor felt something strange—a new softness in his mind, like liquid silk flowing through his brain. He could feel Lacey's thoughts more clearly than ever, and didn't feel like he was a sock in a dryer. He almost felt… feminine.

"Okay, that's weird," he said, as he walked over to the floor-to-ceiling window and gazed out on Tokyo. Lacey had been put on the 21st floor, affording a truly towering vista of the city, despite the cluster of buildings stretching toward the sky. In a way, the wall of structures almost felt like a protective wall—a barrier against the darkness that he knew lurked in the streets below.

"Be glad you can't see them, Lace," he said quietly.

"Who's there?"

Victor perked up instantly. "Lacey?" He spun to see her sitting up on the bed, scooting quickly back toward headboard, her hand groping for anything that might be used as a weapon.

"It's just me, Lacey. Victor." Though the room was

60

unlit, he could see every detail on her face, down to individual freckles that he'd always lovingly thought of as sprinkles of cinnamon. And her eyes—they were even more beautiful than he remembered when he was alive.

Rao nudged him earnestly. *Tell her something that only the two of you know, you dolt.*

"Right," Victor said. By now, Lacey was halfway off the bed, and looking around with a tension just shy of panic. Her hand felt its way across the tabletop, then clutched the hotel phone. Knowing his time was running out, he bypassed the million memories he was sifting through, opened his mouth, put on his best singing voice, and went for it.

"With or without you, with or without *you…*" The words gushed out, him dragging out the notes just the way he knew Bono would have. Lacey jumped, and her eyes seemed to lock right on to him. He stopped singing, and took a quick step toward her, his arms coming up for a hug. "I've missed you so—"

Without warning, Lacey flung the desk phone handset at him. He flinched instinctively, but it stopped before even reaching the foot of the bed, held fast by a cord that refused to stretch clear across the room, and dropped limply to the floor.

"Well, that was a nicer greeting than you gave me two weeks ago," he said.

Lacey's eyes widened. "V-Victor?" Suddenly, she was sure of it—she could see her dead ex standing not ten feet away. More accurately, she could see *through* her dead ex.

He smirked. "In the flesh, baby. Well… not really."

And with that, Lacey promptly fainted.

*

Lacey was certain she was dreaming. Dreaming about Lucky Charms and tabby cats and Victor. Why Victor?

Then again, why not? A pang took her heart at the sudden thought that he was dead. She still had so much to do she wasn't sure she had time to properly grieve the loss. Instead, she decided it would be best to get a good night's sleep so she could help Nainai in the morning.

The dirty orange light that filtered through the window told her it was morning already. She looked herself over— everything was fine. Whatever scare she'd had last night must have been part of her dream. Grateful she hadn't been the target of an intruder, she yawned and blinked, and stretched luxuriously. Maybe a good, hot bath to start the day; she'd noticed a complimentary bath bomb on the tub when she'd first come in. The whole idea sounded divine, and she had no qualms about at least starting the day well.

She'd leave for home the day after tomorrow, and she was planning on spending most of today with Nainai. In her heart of hearts, she knew she may never see the old woman again after this trip, unless she could somehow convince her grandmother to come home with her. But if not, she counted her blessings that her grandmother had still been alive this time around, when KZTB had sent her back for a follow-up piece on a story she'd done over the summer... back when she and Victor were still a thing.

"We still could be a thing, you know," he said.

She gasped and hugged herself instinctively. Victor, who had been standing guard all night, had settled into the desk chair and was watching her from across the room. He had to admit to himself that he'd always enjoyed spooking her from time to time. He hadn't meant for it to be *quite* this literal, however.

Scurrying up against the headboard, she pointed an accusing finger at Victor. "Who are you and why do you look like my dead ex-boyfriend?"

"One question—can you see Ms. Tibbits as well?"

Lacey opened her mouth to speak, but the utterly nonsensical question was not the creepy, stalker threat she had anticipated. She paused, her heart hammering in her chest, and actually gave it a moment's thought. Squinting at the vaguely translucent image of the man who'd once compared her to the giant moth monster from Godzilla (and thought he was complimenting her), she frowned deeply. "I don't see anyone else. Just tell me who you are. Better yet, get out of my room before I call the cops." She reached for her cell phone, but noticed it on the desk next to her crazy hallucination. Her hand shot out to grab the hotel phone.

"It's on the floor, Lace," Victor said. "You sort of threw it at me last night. I guess I freaked you out pretty bad. Sorry about that."

Lacey continued to back away, scooting off the bed, and toward the door to her room. She formulated an escape plan in her mind and began counting down. *3…2…1… now!*

Whirling, she bolted for the door, only to find Victor standing right in front of it.

"Yeah," he said with a smirk, "I move pretty quick now. Even being dead has its perks if you look for them."

Lacey couldn't help but shriek.

"Whoa, whoa, whoa!" Victor said, worried that she might wake half the floor. "Calm down, please. I promise I'm really Victor, and I promise I'm not going to hurt you." Slowly, carefully, he eased out of her way and gave her some space. Gesturing at the door, he smiled kindly. "There. I'm not going to stop you. I know this must be totally freaky for you."

"That's putting it mildly," she said, her knees trembling in the most embarrassing manner. She was grateful she'd slept in her clothes, and even more grateful that she hadn't actually made it into the bath. Had this insanity happened there, with her in all her glory, she wasn't sure how she would have dealt with it.

"I should say something about you in a towel," Victor

said, "but I won't. Come to think of it, I never have seen you in a towel."

"Get out," Lacey said quietly. "Please, just… whatever you are, stop talking to me, stop haunting me, stop making predatory comments."

Victor sighed. This was not the happy reunion he'd planned. He still wasn't entirely sure what he'd said or done, but somehow he'd figured out whatever puzzle Rao had alluded to, and now Lacey could see and hear him. He wanted to jump for joy, watch twenty-four straight hours of Godzilla films, take Lacey in his arms and fly into the clouds and do barrel rolls. Those dreams exploded when she had shrieked. And now, he felt confused fear radiating from her like waves of heat. He knew he had to act quickly. Once again, he decided to just go for it.

"I need you, Lacey."

Lacey had heard that line a few times in her life; usually when a guy had had a few, and figured she was equally off-kilter. The line had never worked, and it wasn't working now. Not daring to make an attempt to retrieve her personal effects—all still set on the desk—she hurried to the door and frantically undid the locks. Just as she was opening it and making for safety, five words stopped her.

"I died, last night, Lacey."

*

Being an investigative journalist meant that Lacey had come across some really tall tales before. But as she paced in front of the rumpled mess of her hotel bed, trying hard to pretend Victor wasn't transparent, or that she wasn't in need of serious medications, Lacey contemplated one of the wildest stories she thought she'd ever hear.

Her brow furrowed, she looked up at Victor through narrowed eyes. "Let me get this straight. You, like an idiot, tried cooking for me."

Victor shrugged. "I'd been taking classes online. You should have tried the sashimi roll I made two weeks back. No one died from it. No pun intended."

Lacey rolled her eyes, but otherwise pretended he hadn't spoken. "Then, you drank some wine—wine you assumed *I* bought, without taking even a second to ask whether I'd buy you wine in the first place, let alone cheap wine—"

"Hey, I just thought you were being nice. Sheesh. Kill a guy for assuming someone's acting kind."

Rao groaned beside Victor. He ignored it.

"As I was saying, you assumed—*assumed*—I had no taste in spirits—"

Victor laughed aloud at that and, after a moment, Lacey got the joke. She glared at the man (she refused to think of him as a ghost). "See, Victor, this is why we fell apart in less than two months. You'd never take anything seriously. You're… you're *dead*, and you're not even serious about *that*."

"Funny thing is," he said, standing with ease, and striding across the entire room in a single, gliding step, "I feel almost more alive now than I did before. Except that I can't really taste or smell anything. Or feel anything. That's kind of lame. But I *am* taking this seriously. You're the one who continued with the dead guy jokes."

"Look," Lacey said, holding her hands up, "I'm done with this. You're the one who came to *me* for help. I've got a flight home in two days, and I may need to pack my grandmother's entire apartment and shuttle her across the Pacific as well. I'm not about to stay here and let you drag me around Japan trying to find some random person in the middle of almost fourteen million people. I came here to follow up on a story and—" She stopped suddenly, choking back an involuntary sob before it escaped.

Victor was suddenly beside her, and she could actually feel, much to her surprise, just the barest whisper of a touch as his arms came around her. "You're worried about your grandma. I know. Man, I wish I could really hold you," he said, resenting the fact that his throat wasn't closing up with the rising sadness he felt. That was a part of life he hadn't expected to miss.

Lacey said nothing, but Victor could feel everything she wasn't saying. After a moment, she regained her composure, and felt her cheeks flame just a touch; she decided not to explore how much of that was caused by her embarrassment of having nearly cried in front of Victor, and how much of it was his nearness which, despite his... situation... still managed to stir something inside of her.

You big stud, you, Rao said, nudging Victor again. He shoved her away, and she pretended to fly out of control and smack into the far wall, whereupon she slid down it with a faked groan.

Lacey squinted at Victor's antics. She wondered whether death had made him insane. He kept claiming his dead pet cat was with him. "I'm going back to America, Victor. Soon. Since you don't seem to have any pressing needs anymore, then I wish you the best in figuring out what happened." She found herself struggling to say the words. Though Victor was a clown, and though she was glad they'd broken up sooner than later, she still cared for him the way one cared for a favorite stray dog. And, if she were truthful, he actually was a very good guy; much better than some of the ones she worked for. If only he'd been a bit more grounded, a bit more grown-up. *Why can't there be just* one *guy who's not fundamentally flawed?* she asked herself.

"You know I can hear everything you're thinking, right?" Victor reminded her.

Lacey tried not to blanch, and in an instant frantically collected all her thoughts into a tiny ball, like a load of dirty laundry, and hurled them into the hamper of her subconscious.

"You're really cute when you play tough, Lace. It's one of the things I love about you. Anyway, I'll come with you."

Lacey's retort died on her lips. She paused, and then straightened, acting non-plussed. "Well I don't suppose you have a ticket, now, do you?" Pausing again, she flicked a sidelong glance at him. "You're about to tell me you don't need a ticket because you're invisible to everyone but me, aren't you?"

Victor smirked. "See, babe? You *do* know me. We'd have been a good pair. I just didn't get enough time to prove it."

Lacey ignored the remark, and tried not to think about the ring she'd found in his charred apartment. The gesture had touched her far more than it should have. "So, why *can* I see you, anyway? I couldn't before last night."

Victor opened his mouth to speak, but only a round, "Uhh…" came out.

Rao cleared her throat beside him, and he looked up to see her settling a pair of spectacles across her nose, and pulling a book literally out of thin air. *When you figured out how to blend with Lacey's mind, you connected with her in a way that's very special. She's not actually seeing* you, *but you're now so closely connected that her* mind *can see, hear, and even just slightly feel you. Well, feel your presence. To her, though, it looks as though you're standing right there. And you can both communicate mind-to-mind, just like I wish you would with me.*

All angels can do this. We just typically don't unless we have permission. It tends to break the rules. As you don't seem all that interested in rules, and as Lacey already sees you, there's not much point—yet—in breaking that connection. Congratulations. You just cheated part of death.

Victor looked at his beloved. "Did you catch any of that, Lace?"

She wrinkled her nose. "Any of what?"

"What Ms. Tibbits—"

Rao! Rao! Rao!

"—what my cat said?"

Lacey sighed. "Fine. I'll pretend your dead cat is here,

too. What did Ms. Tibbits whisper in that cute little ear of yours?"

Rao sighed heavily. *I give up.*

"She said that you and I had a special connection that lets you see and hear me. See? Told you we were a good pair. And…" he paused, and Lacey suddenly felt a ripple of embarrassment from him.

"You were really serious about that ring you bought me, weren't you?"

He nodded sheepishly.

She smiled, and instinctively placed a hand on his shoulder—only to have it pass right through. She hid her blush, and coughed, thinking, *I'm glad we're not doing this when I'm on air.*

"Well, enough of that," he said. "We've got one day left in Tokyo. Whaddya say we do a little sleuthing? You're an investigative reporter for a living. I've seen the way you've snooped around Tokyo looking for the dirt on the scoops you've covered. This is right up your alley."

Lacey clenched her teeth apprehensively. She still had a lot of work to take care of with regards to getting Nainai packed and ready to go. At the same time, part of her actually wanted to know what *had* happened to Victor, but she knew the difference between being a journalist and being a cop. Her command of the Japanese language wasn't even all that good, still, and there were *so* many reasons she should just get on the plane the day after tomorrow and leave it all behind. And yet… maybe for just one day… just to scratch that itch of curiosity…

"I can tell you're thinking about it," Victor said, smiling that dorky smile of his. Lacey felt her heart flutter a bit at the boyish cuteness of it, and promptly chastised herself.

"Am not," she muttered.

"Look," Victor said, "I know you've got your grandma to take care of. Go do that. I'll nose around Tokyo today and tomorrow, and will let you know if I find anything.

We'll all fly home together."

Lacey frowned. "I don't want to have to look all over Tokyo for you when it's time to board the plane."

He smiled, and sauntered up to her. "You won't have to. Now that we're connected, mind to mind, I'm pretty sure I'll be able to figure out where you are." He looked toward his cat. "Right, Rao?"

Rao nodded. *You're actually getting smarter. I'm surprised.*

Victor let the remark go. "Lacey?"

Lacey locked eyes with him, feeling her heart thud a little harder at his tone. *Stop it, Lacey*, she chided herself. *Even if he weren't dead…*

"I just had to see you again. You were worth sticking around for."

It was all Lacey could do to not let her reaction show. She pasted on an "Aww, that's sweet," smile. "Thank you, Victor. You were a good friend." Turning quickly away before her face could betray her, she strode to her suitcase. "So, you go enjoy Tokyo. Check in with me if you find any good leads. I've got a lovely old lady to talk into a long flight."

TEN

The plane ride home, two days later, was strange for Lacey, especially since Victor thought it fun to fly along. He took a window seat... outside. She shook her head for the hundredth time that morning, and glanced back at him floating along as if in an invisible reclining chair, hands behind his head. Not one dark hair on his head shifted in the wind.

A flight attendant rattled a cart of drinks to Lacey. She decided against liquor; she needed all the sensibilities she had, at the moment. Plus, Nainai, although snoring, was sitting beside her. "Just a cranberry, thank you."

Meanwhile, Victor was making the most of being dead. Denial? Perhaps. As he sat there, reclining, he turned to look at Lacey through the window with an occasional smile. She didn't seem too amused. Rao declined the invitation to travel along, since she "had better things to do," though she promised to check in with Victor after the flight.

Victor turned on his side, his knees bent, as if lying on a bed of clouds. He watched as his ex downed a red beverage, hoping his predicament wasn't pushing her to drink. He sighed, looking at her elegant profile. Out of the corner of his eye, he saw a woman walking down the narrow aisle to the bathroom. He glanced up. The woman had a full head of blond hair, bouncing as she went. He couldn't see her face, but he knew that bounce. And, unexpectedly, he could sense her presence.

Jessica?

In the next second, Victor was standing in the aisle, facing the woman. The small chin, the high cheekbones, the man-eating sparkle in her green eyes—yep, it was her all right.

"Okay, so not only did you break into my apartment repeatedly, but you're stalking me on the flight home?" he asked just before her body passed through his, a strange sensation waving through his spirit... and it wasn't good.

One of her passing thoughts grabbed him. *Victor is so dead now. He'll wish he'd never met me.*

He stumbled, and reached for a seat's back to steady himself, but his hand went through. He fell to his knees, and whipped his head around to watch his ex-ex-girlfriend retreat into a lavatory.

Then another strong sensation waved through his body as a cart rattled through him, followed by the flight attendant. That time it wasn't a negative energy, just weird. "I've got to stop letting people walk on me," he said out loud.

Realizing Lacey was a few rows away—and he could indeed yell without causing security to pounce on him like he was loaded with 8 ounces of shampoo—he called out, "Hey, babe! I mean... Lacey!"

The back of her head slightly jerked, so he knew she heard him.

"Lacey, you'll never believe who's on the plane!" He reached her row of seats, and squatted next to her, peeking across the legs of the other passengers in her row.

Lacey's eyes shifted to him, but her face stayed placid.

"It's my ex!"

She rolled her eyes at that.

"What?" He paused, then it dawned on him. "Not you! This is no joke. I mean, you're here, but I'm talking about my *other* ex, Jessica Simcox! Crazy, right? She just walked right through me on her way to the bathroom. She's in there right now." He motioned hastily with a thumb.

Lacey's eyebrows raised to that, and she half stood, glancing back toward the lavatories. He knew she was thinking what he was thinking. Could she of all people have murdered him?

The man closest to Victor crossed his legs, causing a swift kick through his head. "Jeez, man, could you watch it?" he scolded, although that was nothing like full body contact.

"Lacey, we have to find out why she's here! I know it's jumping to conclusions, but I need to know if she's the one! I mean, what are the odds? She stalked me to Tokyo; I'm not sure how she even knew I was there. Then she found my address and broke into my place twice. That's *got* to mean something. And the whole 'To you, my love' note? Totally fits her style."

The man next to Lacey swiftly uncrossed his legs, again swooshing through Victor. "Could you *please* stop that?" Victor narrowed his eyes at him in annoyance, then resumed. "This is our first lead. You and me—we can solve this. The good thing is, she doesn't even know you! You can do that female bonding stuff, start some chit chat after we land, and see what her excuse is for having been in Japan."

Lacey gave him a look, and even without being able to read her mind, he knew it meant, "Could we possibly come up with a dumber idea?"

Flustered, he asked, "Do you have something better than that? I'm all ears."

Lacey pursed her lips, then gave him a smile she knew he couldn't possibly misinterpret.

He took a step back, ignoring the fact that he had just slid his leg through an armrest. "Uh oh. You're going to have fun with this, aren't you?"

Her smile widened, and she nodded.

*

Lacey Ling never was a practitioner of the art of "female

chit chat." But, by Buddha, she'd become one, if need be. She was a journalist. They talk a lot. Why wouldn't this be more of the same? Trailing Jessica down the gangway by about twenty feet, pushing Nainai's wheelchair, while rolling a carry-on suitcase, Lacey's pulse beat faster. She would do it. She would approach the woman, and do so nonchalantly. She wondered why she had expected this would be fun.

Yet she had it all planned out in her mind. They'd both happen to be standing near one another at their designated luggage carousel. Lacey would find a way to offer the stranger a compliment. Maybe something about her red high heels, since they didn't look cheap. Said stranger would give some kind of bimbo giggle and thank her. Then Lacey'd just do it— ask her right out, "What brought *you* to Japan?"

Seven minutes later…

Victor stood a slight distance away, brow furrowed under some serious apprehension. His arms crossed, he gave a curt wave under an elbow for Lacey to get a move on already. Jessica stood, hands on hips, awaiting her suitcase. Lacey moved in closer, a few feet from Nainai, and opened her mouth to speak, but was interrupted by a ringing. Jessica pulled a cell phone, with more bling than Flavor Flav, out of her skinny jeans.

"Hello?" Jessica answered.

In the next instant, Lacey witnessed Victor suddenly flash beside the woman, literally leaning his ear to her phone, almost cheek to cheek.

Lacey sighed. This mission was getting more annoying by the second. How could she possibly compete for attention with a cell phone, especially with Victor plastered to it?

"Yes, for my ultrasound?" Jessica responded. "Yes, I'll be there. Thank you. Oh, of *course* I know who the father is. He's just coming back from Japan. Yes. Yes. Uh huh. Victor St. John, yes. Okay. Bye!"

Victor's jaw dropped emphatically, as he pointed. "She's

pregnant? And she thinks *I'm* the kid's dad? I've never even seen her in a bathrobe, let alone slept with her. Hurry and ask her why she went to Japan."

A group of travelers clamored at the appearance of some luggage. Jessica was one of them. She leaned over and snatched up a leopard-printed suitcase; Lacey saw her last chance.

"Oh, hey," Lacey spoke nearly over the woman's shoulder. "That's… quite the suitcase." *Crap*, she thought. *That was an ambiguous compliment, almost sounding more like an insult.*

Jessica turned to Lacey, tilting her head with a confused look.

"I mean," Lacey hurried, "I *love* the pattern. Where on, um, earth did you find it? Maybe I could buy one, you know."

Jessica eyed her up and down. "Doesn't look like your style," she said simply.

That's when Victor popped in-between them, speaking to Lacey. "Tell her it looks Italian. She raved about it when she bought it. I remember."

Stepping aside slightly, to see Jessica, Lacey quickly said, "It's Italian, right?"

"*French*," Jessica cocked a thin brow.

Victor interjected, "I meant French!"

Lacey gave an awkward laugh, wanting to strangle Victor. "Of course. Italian, French—the two are so similar. Fashion capitals of the world."

Jessica looked overly bored with the comment.

"And actually," Lacey thought of the perfect segue, like any proper journalist, "Japan is competing in the world of fashion. Is that what brought you to Japan to begin with? Are you a model?"

"If you're trying to hit on me," Jessica tossed some hair behind a shoulder, "you're barking up the wrong tree. Besides, I'm taken."

Now Lacey was mad. She wanted to kick a hole in her *French* luggage. She clenched her jaw, but thought better than to berate the murder suspect. "You're taken? Darn it. You got me." She feigned seriousness. "Who's the lucky man?" Oh, that felt creepy. She'd take another shower that afternoon.

Victor's eyes went wide at her.

"Like I'd tell you. Wouldn't want you to stalk him."

Victor muttered, "*She's* one to talk…"

"Is it Victor?" Lacey blurted.

Jessica paused, her face turning a shade of angry red. "I have to go, if you'll excuse me." She turned with a whip of her hair, the quick clacking of her heels echoing as she left.

Victor stepped beside Lacey. "You did good."

"Really?" Lacey huffed. "I've been an investigatory journalist, and yet the most information gathered was from her phone call… which *you* overheard, not me. I can do better than that."

"That woman can't be trusted," Nainai cut into her thoughts, sitting patiently in her wheelchair nearby.

"Huh?" Lacey turned to her. "Why do you say that?" she asked, truly interested.

"I heard her talking to her lady doctor about being pregnant with Victor's child." She shook her head. "Now I may not know Victor *that* much, but what I do know is he would never go that far with someone like that."

Victor stepped right beside Lacey, and with a satisfied smile said, "Did I ever tell you how much I like your grandma?"

Lacey frowned. "That was a bust. I could chase her, but I don't want to be escorted out of the airport by security."

Nainai smiled strangely. "What possessed you to start talking to her in the first place, dear?"

Lacey pursed her lips. "I think you may be more right about 'possessed' than you know."

Her grandmother took her hand. "Well, people who talk to themselves the way you were doing, just now, often have secrets that most of us don't know. You're not too young to be crazy. Confucius say, 'Dead boyfriends make for best conversation. They always understand and agree with you.' I am so sorry you lost him."

Lacey bit her lip, not wanting to say any of the many things Nainai's words had sent swirling in her mind. Victor, for his part, actually *did* seem to understand Lacey's feelings, and she could see the sympathy written on his face.

At last, Lacey got it together. Moments later, her luggage appeared, with Nainai's close behind it. She gathered the heavy bags, ignoring Victor's excuses for not helping, and took hold of her grandmother's wheelchair. "Let's get you home, Nainai."

Victor fell in next to her. "Lacey? I think I should trail Jessica. Something's obviously screwy. I *know* I'm not the father of her child. And why was she in Japan anyway?"

Lacey screwed up her nose. *I have no idea, Victor. You saw what just happened.*

"I did, yeah. But don't worry—I just have to sit and listen. Though, if I could freak her out a bit, that might be fun, too."

Lacey rolled her eyes. "You are such a moron, Victor," she muttered.

"You want me to move on?" Nainai asked,

"No, Nainai," Lacey replied soothingly. "I was just talking to myself."

Nainai nodded sagely. "Remember what Confucius just said."

ELEVEN

Victor was never a huge fan of doctor offices. He was even *less* fond of OB/GYN offices. He knew enough about what *probably* went on that he knew he didn't want to know. Once, at a coffee shop, he had accidentally overheard a couple women discussing something to do with oven mitts and a cold, metal grabber. He got his coffee to go, that morning.

And so he gritted his teeth outside the small clinic, watching Jessica disappear through the front door. The tension was just as real, dead, as when he had been alive, but he no longer had any muscles to relax, and he couldn't do anything to control his breathing.

Odds were, Jessica wasn't *actually* crazy enough to kill him, but to find that he was being blamed for her *pregnancy*? He was just glad he wasn't around to have to worry about it. Only he *was* still around, and he *did* worry about it. With a sigh, he closed his eyes and made his way after her.

The place looked like any other medical office, except that the magazines all had covers of women in various stages of pregnancy and undress. He turned away, grateful he was no longer subject to queasiness. Under the circumstances, the beauty of pregnancy was lost on the thought of being framed by a psycho ex.

Jessica was standing at the counter, looking as stylishly fake as ever, while a receptionist handed her a form and asked her basic questions which Victor pretended he couldn't hear. Instead, he wondered what had actually happened. He'd figured out, pretty early in his time dating her, that she was the kind of girl his mom had warned him about. He'd been hard pressed to resist her advances more than once, and it didn't surprise him to think she'd suckered some other guy—probably even the same night Victor had finally wised up and dumped her. If she were actually pregnant, though, his heart went out to her and to her future child.

Jessica took a seat to fill out some paperwork, and Victor tried probing her mind. She *had* stalked him to Tokyo, and she *had* managed to get into his apartment, somehow; his landlord never did change the locks after that, despite Victor's insistence. Though Rao had proven impeccably honest and annoyingly correct, Victor thought it was possible that the cat might still not have all the facts. So it was that Victor merged on to the insane freeway of Jessica's thoughts, only to exit immediately under a whirlwind of thoughts and images of pregnancy and related matters; though he did pick up something about a one-night stand.

"Okay," he said, "that was more about Jessica's secrets than I *ever* wanted to know." And so, he paced around the office until the time came that Jessica was called back to see the doctor.

Victor hesitated again; suspicious of what he may see or hear if he followed her. Odds were, he wasn't going to learn anything more about his death; but there was a good chance he could learn about who was to blame if she were pregnant. He wasn't sure why he cared, but a morbid curiosity drove him. Before he could talk himself out of it, he shut his eyes and forced himself forward. He slipped through the door behind her, bracing himself for something that might be horrible enough to make him prefer Legion.

All too soon, Jessica had changed into a patient gown, and

seated herself at the edge of the examination table. Her hands clamped together so tight, Victor imagined her false hot pink nails literally popping off.

The doctor, a woman with short gray hair and kind eyes, knocked before entering, then promptly took her place on the rolling stool. "How are you?" she asked. "Seeing you for something other than your checkup, I see?"

"I'm pregnant," Jessica squeaked through clenched teeth. "I took like a bajillion pee tests, and they all came up positive."

Victor stepped back into his corner further, self-conscious that he could quite possibly be seen standing there, as nothing more than a creepy stalker. With that thought, he remembered one of the times Jessica stalked him. He felt his mind float into the past...

Another day, like any other at Kyoto Consulting, had passed. He stumbled through his door, ready to flop on the couch. He loosened his tie as he entered the living room, and who was sitting there? Jessica, wearing nothing but a sequined slip negligee.

Jumping back in surprise, he nearly knocked a picture off the wall. "Gah—*what are you doing here?*"

"I know you missed me." She seductively curled a blond tendril around her finger. "I'm just here to give you what I know you've always wanted."

Victor put a hand up in protest. "*What?* I'm not interested I—I never pushed you for *that* anyway, Jessica."

Undeterred, she stood, slinking toward him, one bare foot in front of the other, with a sway to her hips. Coming right up to him, she said with a husky voice, "Come on, Victor. I flew all the way from Washington to see you. You don't need to play hard to get." With that she put a hand around his neck and stepped on her toes for a kiss.

He turned on his heels, heading back to the door. He opened it, and said, "I have a girlfriend, Jessica. Now please. I'm sorry you wasted a plane ticket, but this is not going to happen."

"A girlfriend?" Her eyes turned red, as she picked up a bag of her belongings. "Well, we'll see how long this one lasts. What's her name?"

Was that a threat? he wondered. Instead of answering, he quickly offered her the chance to change in the bathroom, before leaving.

"No thanks." Her green eyes turned icy as she stepped into the hall.

Jessica's doctor burst his memory bubble. "Go ahead and lie down," she instructed for the ultrasound. The woman soon showed Jessica an image across a small screen. Something flickered. A heartbeat. "You see it? A nice strong beat."

Jessica nodded, with a small smile, appearing reassured. But she said, "I don't know if I'm ready for this."

"What does the dad think?" the doctor asked, nonchalantly.

She shrugged. "I—I don't even know his name. Jeff, Justin? Started with a J. We met at a mixer. I was waaaay too drunk."

The woman eyed her sympathetically.

"But!" Jessica pointed a finger with determination. "I'm seeing someone else... Victor's his name."

Victor's eyebrows shot up at that. He stepped closer. "You're not seeing me." He would've chuckled at the double meaning, if the circumstances were... different.

"And," Jessica went on, "I think he'd make the perfect father."

A dimpled grin unexpectedly sprang across Victor's face. He might not care for Jessica, but the sentiment was somewhat touching.

Breaking the sweet moment, his double-ex-girlfriend said, "He's going to make a ton of money. Just graduated college, and will be able to buy the little bub whatever its heart desires."

Even the doctor physically cringed at that revelation. "Well," she stammered, "there are other... avenues... you can take, if you're not ready. Have you spoken with a counselor about abortion?"

That got an eye roll from Victor, and a "no" from Jessica

None too soon, the appointment was over, and Victor breathed the proverbial sigh of relief as he all but ran from the OB's office. He'd actually left as soon as the doctor had exited, uninterested in seeing where Jessica went from there. He consoled himself with the idea that the visit wasn't a waste, because he was now certain of two things: that Jessica *was* pregnant—and, of course, with someone *else's* child—and Jessica didn't murder him, despite her creepy habits of breaking and entering.

TWELVE

The orange drapes were thin, gauzy. Lacey struggled to pull the fabric over the curtain rod just purchased from Bed, Bath and Beyond.

"Careful, careful," Nainai said, still in the wheelchair. "Don't rip it. I knew we should have taken the rod with us."

"It wouldn't fit in our luggage," Lacey said, now lightly plucking at the material in an effort to scoot it across. "I filled one suitcase alone with about fifty pounds of tea sets and trinkets."

"You'll be happy we did. Quite a few of those bring good luck! I'd like my maneki-neko"—she spoke of the big, paw-waving ceramic cat—"to have the best placement, here, in the living room. How much do you know about feng shui?"

"Not much," Lacey said, distracted. She got the drapes across half the rod.

"I see I have lots of work to do, then." Nainai peered across the large living space, stylishly decorated with a white leather couch set, 60-inch flat screen and pointillism paintings probably from T.J. Maxx. "There's not a drop of Asian inspiration, here."

∗

Victor hated being away from Lacey, but Rao had insisted upon it as soon as the sun had risen, shortly after they'd landed in the States. While the love of his life was off shopping with her eccentric grandmother, Victor was suspended in mid-air over one of the confluence of Interstates 5 and 90 near the heart of Seattle, being mocked by his dead pet. Memories of the odor of car exhaust wafted through his mind; he could hear the honks and curses of the drivers better now than he could when he'd been alive. By rights, he *should* have been grateful that he was up here instead of down there, but he still struggled against the belief that he should be plummeting to his death.

Now, Rao said, waving a paw and causing a rectangular segment of the air to darken into what looked like an old-fashioned chalkboard, *some things you really ought to know since you're so pigheaded that you won't move on with life.*

"Don't you mean 'move on with death'?"

Rao pointedly ignored him, and with another wave of a paw caused badly-drawn chalk images of ghosts to appear on the board. Victor shuddered at the realization of what they meant. *We've already talked about the basics of moving when you're dead. Gravity means nothing. You choose your altitude. Passing through solid objects is automatic unless you come home so I can teach you otherwise. Since you're not coming home, and since I don't have the luxury of loitering with a reprobate like you, the only other* major *lesson I'm allowed to teach you is how to handle the Dark Ones.*

Victor gazed up into the sky, and pretended he was sitting on something solid. "You mean Legion?"

Rao bristled visibly. *That's not a name angels speak. That tends to attract their attention when spoken by spiritual beings. Which leads to the most vital thing I can teach you regarding them: avoidance will be your best defense. If you're never around them, they can never hurt you.*

"And how do I avoid them?"

For starters, you don't call them. Don't use their title. Avoid places they like to congregate—usually dark places, seedy places, and especially situations involving intoxication of some kind.

"So, no back alleys at night, no clubs or bars, and no government buildings."

Rao gave him a half-lidded stare.

"Oh, come *on*, cat. That was funny. You gotta give me that."

She continued as if he hadn't spoken. *Another thing that draws them is negative emotions. They* love *fear, hatred, anger, depression, the whole lot. It's like food for them.*

"But sarcasm is okay, right?"

Rao gave him another withering stare.

"Okay, okay. Geez. Just calling it how I see it."

Rao wiped the board clean. *Angels keep their emotions in check. We're not robots without personalities. There's a difference.* She gestured, and pictures of churches, a copse of trees, and some shrines scrawled themselves across the board.

In the event you're too dumb to avoid them—

"What was that about negative emotion calling them?"

—then your second line of defense is to find a sacred space. Wooded areas can easily go either way, so be careful of them. Better to stick with sites you know are used for holy purposes.

Victor summoned enough courage to look down. He scanned for churches until his fear of falling got the better of him, then whipped his eyes back to Rao. "How about you just show me that super-glowy thing you did when you first saved me from them?"

That, she said, sounding honestly sad, *is something I* cannot *do for you. Not even if you come home.*

Victor stared at her. "You're kidding."

It's a matter of being *holy, Vic. You're a good guy, but you've still got issues to deal with—among them your selfishness and stubbornness. Your unwillingness to sacrifice. You're holding yourself back and, as such, barring* yourself *from becoming the kind of being who can channel the light of truth the way I did.*

It takes courage. Selflessness. Sometimes it helps to have a cause.

"But I *do* have a cause," he said, spreading his hands.

Feel that anger rising in you? she asked.

Victor paused and, on honest reflection, admitted she was right.

You staying here is all about you, *Victor. It's not even really about* her. *And it won't be until you grow up and get over yourself.*

He seethed. "You can read my mind, and you're still saying I don't *love* her? How *dare* you? I would had *died* for her, Tibbits."

Rao sighed. *The fact that you don't even see the problem is part of the problem. But don't worry; I have faith in you. Yes, you do love her, but one day, you'll understand more about what* pure *love is. And when you're there, you won't have to ask me about the "glowy thingy" I do.*

He made to speak but Rao cut him off. *How about we keep working on your ability to fly for now? I can see this isn't the best time to discuss the finer points of your psyche.*

Victor scoffed, but, after a moment, realized he was acting a little too juvenile, and nodded only somewhat sullenly.

That's my boy. Now, there's a redhead down there who's stuck looking for a gypsy with only a jerk for her companion. Let's fly over and see whether we can learn from them before Lacey calls you again. And with that, she was off.

*

Not long after, Lacey stood in the Space Needle, looking out from the observation deck. Confident that her grandma was comfortably settled in with all the food she'd need, Lacey had excused herself for the remainder of the day, and called to Victor's mind, asking him to meet with her again. He'd agreed instantly, and she felt his annoyance at having been separated in the first place; he didn't bother to explain his absence, and she didn't bother to ask.

Cool air fingered her long hair. It was an excellent place to think. At five-hundred and sixty feet above the panoramic view of Seattle, she gazed out at the dull gray sky that loomed above Seattle's distinct cityscape. Normally, the view would have been breathtaking—enough to make her ignore the other few patrons—but she had more important things on her mind. Victor paced in the air nearby, clearly lost in thought.

"This whole finding out who your murderer is, is going to be harder than anticipated," she said. Noticing a sidelong glance from another woman on the deck, Lacey moved elsewhere, Victor trailing her. She stopped, then lowered her voice, hoping that the old man trundling toward her on the observation deck wouldn't have such acute hearing. "We're dealing with two separate continents. Two different cultures!"

"Which is why you'll be my perfect teammate," Victor said, smiling big. "Call it serendipitous!"

She pulled a notepad out of her purse. "We need to make a list of who might've killed you. Tell me who you think may have done it." Poised and waiting, she looked up at Victor, who, for drama's sake, was pacing along the ledge, beyond the metal fence enclosure.

"We know Jessica is no longer a possibility," he said. "She just wanted me to be her baby daddy."

"Right," Lacey agreed with a serious nod. "In that case, she wouldn't want you dead."

"And…" He paused.

"Think of who might have a grudge against you. Did you get into any fights lately? Make someone angry?" The thought was absurd. Everyone seemed to get along with Victor.

"The IRS?" he stated weakly. "I filed for an extension in May."

She huffed. "And you are an accountant? Think, Victor."

"I'm sorry, it's kinda hard to when I know my funeral is this weekend."

Lacey's face softened. "I'm sorry."

"It's going to be really weird seeing my own coffin." His eyes shifted to her. "You'll be there, right?"

"Yes, of course," she said.

Her phone rang. She pulled it out of her slim coat. It was Greg.

"Hello?"

"Hey, Lace. You made it home okay?"

"I did."

"Where are you at, right now?"

"The Space Needle."

"I couldn't reach you for a couple days. I'm very sorry for what happened. We need to talk. Can we maybe meet up tonight?"

"Uh, I'm not sure, Greg." She hesitated, flicking a telling glance toward Victor.

Victor took the hint and walked far enough away to give her the impression of some privacy, then sat on the ledge to let her deal with the uncomfortable phone call without distraction. Being able to dangle on the edge of a structure taller than most skyscrapers without so much as breaking a sweat was an unexpected perk of being dead. High above the traffic and general busyness of Washington's most famous city, Victor found he actually enjoyed the view, even during daylight. He just wished he didn't have to spend his nights holed up against the demons. At least he could enjoy time with Lacey during waking hours.

That won't last forever, Rao said suddenly, materializing. *For your sake, you need to spend more time listening to me and less time dragging your ex-girlfriend into something that could get her killed.*

Victor waved it away while Lacey's call continued. "You didn't seem to have a problem with me doing that in Tokyo." Rao frowned, and turned her back on Victor.

Tokyo had proven disappointing, in the end. Despite his ability to fly, walk through walls, and listen in on conversations because he was invisible and could read minds (and he'd heard some *extremely* interesting things lately), nothing had so much as tipped him off. Meanwhile, Rao had continued to follow him around, laying the guilt on thicker than tar as she tried persuading him it was time to ditch the scene and give Heaven a try. Though she had lain off since his little encounter with Lacey postmortem, she still managed to be annoying, though it was simultaneously comforting to have another familiar face around.

As if mocking Victor, Rao began prancing around the extremities of the Space Needle, flitting out into space now and again, whereupon she'd plummet out of sight, only to reappear moments later. *Do you really think you and Lacey are going to figure this out? I'm telling you again—your time here is done. You really don't know what you're missing.*

"Will you stop doing that?" he muttered, his enhanced eyes still scanning the streets below. "You know I hate it when you pretend to fall from high places. Freaks me out."

You're dead, Vic. You've been flying *yourself. How does this*—and she leapt out into space, dropped a few stories, then rocketed back to his side—*still get to you? You're halfway doing the same thing, dummy.*

Victor ignored her intentional dig, and turned back to his thoughts. Rao, in response, started flying loops and doing crazy dives and twists, even "crashing" into the Space Needle, only to emerge from somewhere else. "Why would someone want to kill me?"

I could think of plenty of reasons.

"Was it something I did? Something I *didn't* do? Whoever it was, they knew where I lived. Who knew where I lived? Lacey, my parents, some friends from home, the human resources department at Kyoto Consulting… and of course Jessica, but I've already ruled her out."

Why did *you keep in touch with her on Facebook, anyway?*

Victor sighed. "She stalked me there, too. I swear I never posted my Tokyo address online, though. And I guess there were still some old habits. Maybe I really thought we could just be friends, even if she was psychotic. But I didn't think she was *actually* clinically insane."

You win some, you lose some.

"Well, yeah," Victor said, standing and deciding to walk carefully along the ledge if only to annoy his cat. His arms still instinctively extended to balance him, but he found the effort was entirely unnecessary. He heard a beep, and turned back to Lacey. Her expression was cold and thoughtful. He looked at Rao, who shrugged.

I don't mind spending time with you, but I've got a lot of things I need to do. If you're not coming home with me, then I'll wish you luck, and take care of business. But don't worry—I'll check in now and again. Just don't expect me to be at your beck and call.

The cat smirked, and Victor felt a strange wave of pleasant condescension coming from her. *I'm going to check on my kittens for a bit. Maybe even a few months, they're so cute. Well, they were cute. Now I enjoy the great grandkids. Toodles.*

"Good idea. I'll handle Lacey." He shot the cat a look before she could make a retort. His old pet glared, instead, and stuck out her tongue, before dissolving into mist.

Victor teleported himself next to his girl. "You okay? What did your boss say?"

She paused, her brow furrowing more. "He's not my boss anymore."

"What? Why? He didn't understand you needed some grieving time? Didn't you tell him the details? Your boyfriend—I mean, ex-boyfriend—was murdered! How inconsiderate can he be?"

"That's not it." Lacey shook her head. A bit of wind spun a tendril of hair over an eye and she wiped it away. "I quit."

Victor's mouth dropped. "But I… What? Lacey, I don't want all this"—he made exaggerated hand motions around his translucent silhouette—"to get in the way of you living your life. It will take some time to cope. God knows I need time! But you can't just quit your *amazing* job over my sudden lack of corporealness."

"Is that a word?" The side of her mouth turned up.

"I don't know. I'm the accountant; *you're* the journalist." He stopped. "Why are you smiling?"

"It will be okay," she assured, a sense of strength shining through her brown eyes.

"This is why women are confusing," he said, gesturing to her. "Am I going to have to dive into more mind reading?"

"Look, Victor, I quit him while in Japan." She started walking, her heels clacking against the concrete, as she headed to the stairwell's door. "He wasn't being totally honest about things. Plus, it will be best for Nainai, at least until I figure out a plan of care for her. I'm thinking, if her condition worsens, I might need a nurse to watch over her when I'm not home. Besides, I've got savings that'll hold me for a while. And my résumé is excellent. I'll find more work again soon."

"He hit on you, didn't he?" They descended the stairs together toward the parking lot, Victor practicing floating, rather than stepping, as he went.

Lacey sighed. "Well, you cut to the chase. I don't know. Maybe a little, but I pretended not to notice. But that wasn't the reason I quit. The reason I quit was dishonesty. He defined 'shady.' I don't even think he ever really intended on giving me a talk show." She gripped the handrail, halting a moment. Some people ascending passed her by.

"Lacey? Why didn't we just take the elevator down?"

She frowned. "Because everyone else would be doing the same thing. The stairs were supposed to be private enough that I could talk to you without looking certifiable."

"That's so sweet," Victor quipped. "Always nice when a hot woman wants to get you alone."

She swatted at him. "Give it a rest. Anyway, I found some evidence having to do with illegal exporting. He let me borrow his laptop since mine was on the fritz… and let's just say I stumbled upon things."

"Things?" Victor raised his eyebrows. "Care to share?"

"Something tells me he was shipping things he shouldn't have to a number of other countries—mostly in Asia."

"Illegal exporting?" Victor scrunched his nose pensively. "Why in the world would he need you for that?"

She frowned. "I don't know. I'm assuming I was some sort of cover for his dealings."

"What was he having exported?"

Lacey pulled up her phone, opened her camera app, and slid to a picture of a bright yellow bird. It was small, its wings caught in motion.

"Birds?" Victor said incredulously. "What the…?"

"Parakeets to be exact. And that's not all." Lacey swiped to a picture of an amber-colored, small bottle.

"And that would be? What? Vanilla?"

90

"No, an aphrodisiac supplement." Lacey frowned.

"Parrots and sex stimulants. I should be less surprised, considering who we're talking about." An image of Greg Mendoza popped up in Victor's mind: half-naked, lying in a room filled with the exotic birds, his chest oiled with an opium love spell. He shuddered. "Well, I'm glad you got out of that when you did. Does this mean we can turn our full attention to figuring out why I'm your new night light?"

Lacey rolled her eyes. "Not quite." She stopped in front of a black Lincoln MKZ, and triggered the locks. "Get in," she said.

Victor complied, and grabbed for the seatbelt by habit, remember immediately how unnecessary that was once his hand went right through it.

"He wants to meet with me tonight," Lacey said, putting on a large pair of sunglasses, and pulling out of the lot.

"You said no, right?"

"No, I said yes. He wants to explain. And I want to wrap up some unfinished business."

"Isn't that what Human Resources is for?"

"Don't worry. It will be quick. I can still work on your case."

THIRTEEN

The chopper's blades sliced the air so loudly Lacey struggled to hear Greg even through the headphones. It was dark out, and they were climbing higher than the Space Needle, a spray of stars seeming to beckon them toward Heaven. Victor sat in the back seat, grateful he didn't have to listen to Rao chastising him. It allowed him time to seethe at the thoughts rolling out of Lacey's recently-former boss, Greg. The man must be an expert pilot to be able to fly so smoothly while simultaneously fantasizing about the woman next to him.

"I'm glad you decided to take me up on my offer to explain myself," Greg said, looking toward Lacey not quite long enough to give himself away. But neither Lacey nor Victor were fooled. "I wanted to talk about, well I wanted to talk about a few things."

Lacey could already smell the charm coming on—his feigned "vulnerability," where he put on his "human" side to make himself seem more boyishly approachable.

"This dude is such a scam artist, Lace," Victor growled. "I'd deck him if I could. You don't even want to know what he's thinking about you. I'm glad you quit your job."

Lacey, for her part, managed to merely grind her teeth and

maintain a professional demeanor while Greg carried on. Seattle passed below them, downtown falling behind as they sped over silent, steel mountains of cargo containers on the piers, and south toward the industrial district.

"You know," Greg said, completely unaware of Victor and his conversation with Lacey, "it's a shame that accountant ex-boyfriend of yours died. Like I said, we could have used him. You may have guessed that KZTB sometimes… struggles… with money. Advertising revenue hasn't been as good, the last three quarters, as usual. It's part of why we wanted to branch out and give you your own show." He shot her a look, and Lacey felt ice run through her veins. "You sure you won't change your mind about resigning?"

Lacey suppressed a shudder. "I'm certain."

Greg frowned lightly, but shrugged. "Suit yourself. But remember—if you ever want to come back…"

Neither Lacey nor Victor needed to read minds to catch his meaning.

"As I was saying, we've been trying to get ourselves back in the black. If my MBA taught me anything, it's that a business model with diversity can get you through some tough times. And so, I helped the station diversify." Just then, he banked hard around, throwing Lacey sideways. She caught herself immediately, just as the helicopter started a quick descent toward a group of buildings by the water.

"Sorry 'bout that." Greg chuckled. "I guess I take out my rush hour frustration in the air sometimes."

Lacey faked a smile. "Of course."

Victor growled behind her. "Get away from this guy, Lace. As soon as you land. Call a cab, or something."

Lacey ground her teeth again, and rebuked Victor mentally. *Have some faith in me, Victor. I'm a big girl. You never did give me credit for that.*

Victor smiled automatically. "Hey! You did it! You broke down and talked to me with your mind again. That's my girl."

Lacey turned her face toward the window so Greg wouldn't ask why she blatantly rolled her eyes. She noticed the helicopter closing on a run-of-the mill warehouse, pier-side. The ugly, gray brick of a structure seemed to be the product of World War II thinking, though, surprisingly, it had a helipad on the roof. Victor glanced down as well, and felt himself grow cold.

"Oh, no. Please, no," he muttered.

Lacey turned around instinctively, sensing his fear. "What's wrong?" she asked.

"Excuse me?" Greg cut in, eying her oddly, before checking the back seat.

Lacey cleared her throat. "I thought I heard some weird noise from the engine compartment. I don't know much about helicopters, and I got worried."

Greg chuckled easily, and patted her knee. "That's okay. I'll take care of you."

Victor growled again, and lunged for Greg, but only succeeded in winding up outside the helicopter. The KZTB manager removed his hand quickly enough that Lacey didn't have to, but she was simultaneously embarrassed and flattered that, even in death, Victor was jealous.

Victor stuck his head back through the canopy. "You need to get out of here, Lacey." Already, dark shapes swarmed up from the warehouse, hissing and wailing as they angled directly for him and the helicopter. He could only imagine what they'd do to Lacey if they got her. "Go *now*."

I kind of can't, Victor, she thought, trying hard to put an edge in her mental tone. *Not all of us can leap tall buildings in a single bound or move through solid objects.*

Suddenly, Victor was looking around frantically. "I can't stay. I need to—aw, *man!*" In an instant, he disappeared from view.

Lacey scowled. *Victor? Victor? What's going on?*

"You okay, Lacey?" Greg said, as the chopper touched down without a bump.

Lacey blinked as her head pivoted, trying to search for Victor without letting on to her growing sense of dread. Something in the air didn't feel right, and it seemed to have gotten much worse since landing. "This is an unfamiliar part of town," she said. "I'm just trying to orient myself."

Greg peered at her a moment. "You do remember covering a story about money laundering in the Industrial District a few months back, right? We're on River Street. *That* River Street, if that helps."

Lacey groaned inside. Of course Greg would have remembered that. "Oh. I guess coming in from the air threw me off a bit."

Greg shrugged, then flipped a few switches, and the roar of the engine faded to a mournful whine that reminded Lacey too much of a banshee. In a fluid motion, he unbuckled, and popped open his door. By the time Lacey had undone her harness, her ex-boss was already opening her door, and extending a hand to help her down. She tried not to bite her lip as she debated taking the hand for show, or simply getting out on her own. She opted for the latter, and nimbly hopped out of the helicopter, skipping right over the step and landing easily despite the fact that she was in heels. The wind from the blades still made a mess of her hair, but she felt something else in that cold, stiff breeze. *Victor*, she thought again. *Where'd you go?*

The lack of response made her shiver.

Greg, hunching against the dying gale of the rotors, placed a hand on her shoulder and directed her toward a stairwell door on the roof. They hurried inside, and down a set of stairs, emerging into a dimly-lit warehouse. Immediately, the smell of the river was replaced by a series of exotic, spicy scents, none of which Lacey could identify. Some smelled superb; others made her nose burn. The usual hum of overhead fluorescents was punctuated by distinct chirping sounds from further on in the warehouse; the noise reminded her of the parakeets she'd once owned. *So this is where Greg keeps them. Why is he showing me this?*

Greg walked over to a shelf laden with small, wooden crates, and gestured. "Lacey, I've got a gift for you."

She stiffened, but did her best not to show it, instead

raising her eyebrows as if curious. "You don't have to get me anything, Greg. And you're *not* going to buy me back into KZTB."

The producer laughed. "I've always loved your spunk and spirit. We're really losing out by losing you. But don't worry, I'm not going to force the issue. This isn't a bribe; just a gift. And to sweeten the deal, you get to pick your gift."

She narrowed her eyes as Greg pulled the top off one of the crates. Inside, packaged in straw, were a dozen or so glass bottles with varicolored liquids, or even powders. Flicking a glance at him, she inched forward. "What are they?" She suspected she already knew.

Greg smiled wide. "Cosmetics. Have a look."

Lacey felt her skin tighten, but Greg took a generous step away from the shelf. Carefully approaching the crate, she gave him a wide berth, keeping an eye on him even as she furtively examined the contents of the box. Something on a label caught her eye, and she lifted one of the bottles gently out of the packing straw. She peered at the label, then turned her eyes on Greg. "Powdered unicorn horn?"

Greg laughed. "Okay, ya got me. Remember what I was saying I'd learned from my MBA? Yeah—this is me 'branching out.' Turns out, there's a good market for 'alternative' cosmetics in Asia. You wouldn't believe the stuff some people buy over there; and I don't just mean products, but *ideas*. Like 'Santa Claus' ideas. That 'powdered unicorn horn'? It's scented talc with a little glitter. Pure placebo, but it sells way better than you'd think. All this," and he waved his hand at the expansive warehouse, "is my stock. I get the stuff from suppliers all over the world. It's staggering how much you can make on the margins as a middle man. And Seattle, being the port city it is, is the perfect place for running an export business. We save *big* by cutting down on over-the-road shipping costs." He smiled proudly. Lacey pretended to be impressed.

"See," he continued, "I got the idea a few months ago when we first visited Japan. In fact, your, uh, old boyfriend kind of clued me into it."

Lacey's jaw dropped slightly. "Victor? Victor has trouble picking out a deodorant scent. What would *he* know about perfumes and cosmetics?"

Greg waved it away. "Friend of a friend, is all. I was just trying to be nice to your man."

She grimaced. "He's not…" She trailed off, fighting the unexpected lump in her throat.

"Oh, geez. I'm sorry," her old boss said, stepping toward her. "That… that was really insensitive of me." He put a comforting arm around her, but Lacey politely stepped away. "I know it's still pretty raw, even if he did walk away from you. He lost big, giving you up."

Lacey bit her lower lip and turned back to the crate of cosmetics. Infusing indifference into her voice, she lightly said, "Can we please not talk about it?"

From the corner of her eye, she saw Greg nod. "Yeah. So, back to business, take a look at these perfumes." He reached past her, his hand uncomfortably close, and pulled free a perfume bottle with amber-colored liquid in it. The label was in Chinese, but had the English words, "Goddess's Delight" beneath it. "Here," he said, offering it to her. "This is one of the more popular ones."

Lacey took the bottle warily, and spent a few moments trying to read the ingredients. Finding that her Chinese was not up to snuff, she decided to test it carefully. Holding the bottle at arm's length, she spritzed the air, then took a shallow whiff. To her surprise, the scent was, in fact, quite heavenly. She sprayed the faintest bit on to her wrist, where it tingled pleasantly, and took a slightly deeper breath. Then another. And another. "Mmm," she said. "This is divine."

"Like it?" Greg asked. "Keep it. It's on me; we build samples and gifts into the profit margin, along with lost and damaged inventory. In fact, why don't you try out some more of these? You can't have them all, but maybe one or two that you really like. And take your time. I want you to really get a vision of what we're trying to do here. I'd like you to really like our products."

She looked sideways at Greg. "I thought you were a television magnate. Not the Avon lady." She was grateful he didn't seem aware of what she'd learned from his laptop; she could do without his suspicion.

He laughed openly. "Man, I'll miss you, Lacey. Not even Debbie has quite your humor or charm. And I mean that."

Lacey knew better than to believe the compliment, but she couldn't help the little flutter of pride in her chest at the comparison. After all, Deborah McMahon hadn't been hand-picked to spearhead an attempt to do a foreign morning show. For the briefest of moments, Lacey began to wonder whether she'd been too rash in quitting KZTB.

She shook her head clear, and selected another bottle of perfume, ignoring the warnings in her head. With another spritz and a breath, she found a second scent that she liked. The third bottle was too bitter for her tastes, the fourth a bit too "old woman," but the fifth was even better than "Goddess's Delight." Before she knew it, she had sampled a couple dozen perfumes from various boxes, and found it was getting difficult to stop. The fragrances called to her in alluring ways. She felt warm inside, heady, and *alive*.

Greg was right—he'd make a *killing* off this stuff. She could smell it all day and never get tired of it. On and on she went, moving from perfumes to eye shadow, mascara, and a rainbow of nail polishes. She even tried some of the "powdered unicorn horn" with a surprisingly girlish giggle.

When she turned back toward Greg, she couldn't help but notice just how *handsome* he was. How had she not seen that? His smile seemed to gleam, and his eyes were *gorgeous*. She asked herself why she'd ever shied away from him, and, in fact, when he stepped toward her and reached past her to take another product—facial cream—out of the crate before her, she shivered with delight when his hand brushed hers.

"Pretty good stuff, isn't it, Lace?"

Without thinking, she found herself nestling slightly against him. One of his hands touched her shoulder, while the other handed her the tub of facial cream. She looked at it, giggled again, and tossed it aside, ignoring the sound of it hitting the concrete behind her. "You've been holding out on me, Mister Mendoza," she said, turning fully around to look up into his eyes; they really *were* mesmerizing. "All this time, you had so much more depth than I ever knew. You shouldn't be *behind* the camera, you should be center stage."

A swooning sensation swept her mind, and she suddenly caught a hint of a new scent, this time coming from Greg. She placed her hands on his chest and leaned in close to smell his collar. "Mmmm," she said, drawing back only partially. "You are a man of *so* many surprises."

Vaguely, something in the back of her mind was screaming at her to get away—to flee from this guy. Warnings of deception cried out, but she casually shoved them away. She'd been confused, earlier. Blinded by emotions. Yes, she'd miss Victor, but Victor had been a boy. Greg Mendoza was a *man*. A married one, perhaps, but things could change. A new wave of heat rushed through her, mingling with the musky call of his scent. His hand came up to the small of her back, and she burrowed her face into his neck, breathing deeply like a drowning woman coming up for air.

"I have a business proposition for you," Greg murmured into her hair. "I know you said you want to leave KZTB, but Lacey—I don't know how we'll make it without you. You were a *hit* in our trial runs in Japan. I hate to beg, but I'd triple your salary if it'd convince you to stay. And with your savvy, I think you'd be the perfect choice for the producer of the show there."

"And how," she asked playfully, "will a station verging on bankruptcy afford to pay me triple?"

Greg smiled and stroked her head. "We're going to make a little fortune in the cosmetics business. You'd make an *excellent* business partner. And the good thing about Asia is there's no drug war there. And they're a bit more… reasonable… about their government oversight, if you know how to go about things."

He held her at arm's length, and she felt herself getting lost in his piercing blue eyes. "With your talent, you'd be a *killer* saleswoman. And with your looks, you'd be the perfect model, especially for an Asian market. You and me, Lacey. We'll take on the world. Whaddya say?"

"I say," she said, tilting her chin up ever-so-slightly and reveling in the emotions coursing through her, "that we should *definitely* consider it. And," she walked her fingers up along his chest, ignoring the continued screams of protest from deep inside her skull, "that we might want to consider a few other things. Perhaps starting with dinner?"

A beautiful smile spread across his face, and Lacey felt her breath catch. Her lips pursed of their own accord, and her eyelids fluttered halfway closed. She leaned forward, half wondering what she was doing, knowing that this was *so* wrong on *so* many levels, and yet almost unable to help herself. Fire and ice warred inside her, driving her on through the intoxicating haze of the perfume and cologne. She wanted this. *Needed* this. Greg seemed to need it as well. His eyes closed, and he began leaning in purposefully, his lips angling toward hers.

"*Mendoza-san!*"

Like a light switch being flipped, Lacey was snapped out of her trance. She and Greg practically leapt apart, and the lovely fog her mind had been swimming in seemed to evaporate into a faint, sickly mist. Lacey shook her head clear, and wondered, with horror, what she had almost done. A staccato slap of footsteps on concrete caught her attention, and she pivoted to see a stocky Japanese man striding toward them. Fierce-looking dragon tattoos wrapped around his thick arms; his face seemed set in a permanent scowl; to top it off, he seemed to be shrouded in an almost palpable darkness, something that sent shards of ice through Lacey's innards. Though she felt she should be able to place him, nothing distinctive came to mind. She hid her urge to swallow hard.

"Mendoza," the man spat, "why do you insist on wasting product?"

Greg swept his arms wide as if to embrace the man, and put on his most charming smile. "Kombanawa, Orochi-san. You're here early."

"Cease the pleasantries," the Japanese man barked, before turning his eyes on Lacey. Lacey felt him practically dissecting her, but rather than the hunger she saw in most men's eyes, she saw cold calculation, as if she, too, were more "product." He scowled. "Who is the woman?"

The TV guru patted his friend's back; the man shrugged it harshly away. "Where are my manners?" Greg said grandly. "Orochi, allow me to introduce the lovely Lacey Ling." The man called "Orochi" sniffed with disinterest. "Lacey Ling, allow me to introduce Mister Orochi Watanabe, a close business associate of mine, and my Asian counterpart in this endeavor." Lacey hesitated, then extended a hand to shake. Watanabe eyed it, but didn't take it. After an awkward moment, Lacey folded her arms, and returned the man's scowl. She wasn't about to be cowed by some stranger with a bad attitude.

"We must speak," Watanabe said to Greg, not taking his eyes off Lacey. "Privately."

Greg gave Lacey an apologetic smile. "Sorry, Lace. Business stuff. But hey—think about my offer. Three heads are better than one. For now, you can head back to see the birds if you want." Watanabe's eyes flashed, but Greg gave him a soothing look, and the Japanese man said no more. Lacey, still struggling with the realization of what had nearly happened, quickly excused herself and retreated further into the warehouse.

The twittering birds grated at her. As beautiful as they were, there was something about their ceaseless screeching that got to her. And yet, she welcomed the distraction from the creeping sense of… whatever it was coming from the Watanabe guy.

"Victor," she said quietly, through the tap-tap of her heels and enough bird noise to drown out normal conversation. And yet, he didn't answer. *Victor*, she repeated in her mind, trying to "think loudly," and not knowing quite how to do that. Still, she heard nothing from him. Instead, chilly tendrils seemed to weave through her mind, and she shuddered, wrapping her arms around herself for warmth.

Glancing behind her, she could only barely make out Greg and his companion. Ducking around a corner, into what appeared to be another room, she stopped. Row upon row of shelving was covered in bird cages, far more than she had imagined. Even from outside the room, the cloying stink of parakeet poop wafted out on a fine layer of dust that made her sneeze almost as soon as it touched her nose. Something seemed off about the birds. Squinting, she saw that their eyes looked strange; almost milky. Stepping closer, she noticed that several of them had some kind of goop oozing from their eyes. She made a disgusted noise.

As if they all heard her at once, the birds broke into a cacophony. She covered her ears and backed hurriedly out of the bird room, only to find the two men walking toward her. Acting as casual as possible, she slipped back into the noise, and decided to look for another way out. Maybe there was another stairwell to the roof. She could just go upstairs and wait for Greg. Or, better yet, take Victor's advice and just call a cab. Jogging past the cages, soon coughing on the dust, Lacey reached the far wall only to find it stacked high with more wooden crates, each one bearing a small cluster of photographs.

Curious, she stepped up to one, and noticed a starving little Japanese girl staring back from the picture. The caption, as best she could translate, alluded to poverty and… darker uses for children, the kind no one ever talked about. She gasped, and placed a hand on her chest. Almost against her will, she looked at another crate. This one showed a cluster of children in a similar state as the first girl. The words didn't hint at slavery, but even without them, it was clear the children were in dire need of help. Scanning the crates quickly, she found they all seemed to be the same.

She wondered what was in the crates. Was it food supplies

for the kids? Clothing and toiletries? Or was it something worse? Was it the children *themselves*? She took a deep breath, regretting it instantly, as she launched into another spat of coughing and sneezing. When it subsided, she told herself she was just being paranoid and, before her nerves got the best of her, reached to open a crate.

It was nailed closed. She tried another, with the same results. Looking over her shoulder, she saw that she was still alone, and turned back to the crates. They all seemed to be nailed shut. Casting about, she found nothing that was likely to serve as a crowbar. Frowning, Lacey reined in her investigative instincts and made a mental note to get the address for this place. She'd come back with the proper tools and find out what Greg was keeping in the crates. Turning quickly, she made for the door.

She was nearly to it when Watanabe stepped through from the main warehouse area. His eyes narrowed instantly, and he moved toward her with purpose. She wanted to run, to scream, or to whip off her heels and attack him. Instead, she strode straight toward him, face tight, jaw set. He reached for her, but she quickstepped past him like she owned the place. Watanabe was quicker. A powerful hand crushed her bicep and jerked her backward.

"Why are you here?" he demanded.

Lacey whirled on him, but refrained from slapping him. "Take your hand off a lady." She tugged hard, but he only tightened his grip. "Greg Mendoza is a personal friend. I don't think he'll take kindly to the idea of his business associate mistreating me."

He yanked her close and seized her other wrist. "Empty threats do not frighten me, Miss Ling. Mendoza-san will not protect you from your own idiocy."

"I said let *go*," she hissed, ramming her foot sideways into his shin. He grunted in pain, then slapped her hard enough to spin her around. She stumbled into a wall, blinking away the stars. Before she could orient herself, she lunged for the door—barely dodging Watanabe's grab—and out into the open. "Greg? Greg!"

The man's head appeared from behind a shelf a stone's throw away just as the Japanese businessman snatched her left arm a second time. "Yeah, Lacey?"

"Mister Watanabe wanted to show me around. Care to join us?" Watanabe growled beside her and dug his fingers in. She held back a wince, and jerked forcibly away, finally breaking his grasp.

"Orochi's good. He knows the place. I've got a couple things I'm looking at over here."

Lacey put on her "sexy pout" face, and a tone to match. "Please, Greg? It would mean *so* much to me."

Greg looked side to side, scratched his neck, and shrugged. "Uh, yeah. Sure. Why not?"

Beside her, the stout Asian man growled again. "Do not let yourself be confident in your sense of safety, Miss Ling." With that, he turned and walked quickly back into the parakeet room.

Sighing inside, Lacey smiled as Greg reached her. Taking his hand, she allowed him to lead her around the whole facility.

*

The helicopter ride home was practically boring after the night's events. Greg had apologized profusely for Watanabe's behavior and "condemned in the strongest possible terms" the fact that the man had slapped her, promising that he'd have a "little talk" with his associate.

"Not to change the subject too much," he continued, "but what'd you think of my little aviary?"

Lacey took a thoughtful breath. "I hated them. It's why I got rid of my pet parakeets as a child."

Greg laughed. "Not the answer I was hoping for, but to be honest, I don't like them much either. Turns out, certain Asian markets are *glutted* with them, and I get them at bargain basement prices. I ship them their aphrodisiacs, then they ship me their birds. Great profit margins both directions. It's easy to sell parakeets anywhere in the country."

"As delicacies?" she teased, trying to keep him off balance.

Greg laughed again. "No, as pets. C'mon, Lace. You know me better than that. Would I *really* invite you into a business that wasn't totally above board?"

She gave him a smile to cover her thought of, *Why do you think I left KZTB?*

"Already the first quarter's profits are in. They're even bigger than we expected—and we haven't even tapped a tenth of the potential market. I tell you, we're going to go so big with this that KZTB will almost be an afterthought."

Lacey turned to look out the window. "I bet you'll do a lot of charity write offs, too, right?"

A strange wariness crept into his tone. "Of course. Why do you ask?"

She shrugged. "I remember seeing homeless people when I was in Japan. And I've read articles about human trafficking across Asia, and beyond." She locked eyes with him. "Even of little children."

Greg studied her for a moment, then smiled casually. "You always were so astute, Lacey. And yes, I noticed them when I was there, myself. In fact, Orochi Watanabe is helping me fight that kind of thing. His firm has connections, and—don't tell him I told you this—his own sister was, shall we say, 'sold' twenty years ago. Ever since then, well… he's had an agenda."

Lacey's stomach lurched. She hadn't even considered the man's past. Though he clearly had no idea how to treat a woman, losing a sister to something worse than death certainly would sour a person. "You know," she said, deciding to take a different tack, "I'd have an easier time getting behind ending human trafficking than I would just selling cosmetics. I'm flattered that you think so highly of me," and she didn't miss the quick examination he gave her, "but I'd rather feel like I was standing for something. You know what I mean?"

Her former boss nodded carefully, and drifted the helicopter down over the taller buildings in Seattle. Already,

CLAIRE KANE & STAN CROWE

Lacey thought she could see the helipad lights at KZTB. She held her breath as they made the final descent, hoping Greg wasn't planning her any harm. She'd probably shown her hand more than she should, and his wariness was barely hidden. Though she thought him morally bankrupt, she knew he wasn't stupid. Still, she wasn't an idiot herself; Greg could be outmaneuvered with a little careful thought. And that involved making sure *he* wasn't thinking so carefully.

She briefly considered trying to capitalize on whatever mistake she had made in the warehouse, but the mere memory of being close to him made her skin crawl. She did, however, take his proffered hand after they set down, and he hurried over to get her door. As she stepped down, he took both her hands in his; it took all her willpower to not pull away.

"Sorry again about Orochi," Greg said. "Thanks for taking time to hear me out. I know things have been pretty rough on you, especially with your ex. Were you two... close?"

Lacey bit her lip and looked away, allowing him to take that however he would. Greg baited, and reached up to stroke her face. "It's hard to lose someone you love. I can't make up for him being gone, but hopefully," and he flicked a glance to the side, "I've given you some things to think about tonight." He locked eyes with her, and she could tell he was still dwelling on what had almost happened in the warehouse.

"Sure you won't come back to work? I'll give you a week's paid bereavement leave, just because. Think about what I said—the show, you as a producer, that cause you were talking about. We could do great things for the station. For *us*."

She cringed inside at the way he said "us," but kept her reaction measured. "Let me sleep on it, Greg. Thanks for the ride back to the station."

"Hey, beats walking clear from the industrial district." He chuckled lightly, and Lacey gave him a courtesy smile as she stepped away.

She could tell he was hoping for at least a peck on the cheek, but she wasn't about to honor that. "Goodnight, Greg. I'll be in touch." She turned quickly away and strode for her car. She wasn't sure how well she'd sleep on anything, tonight. *Where are you, Victor?*

No response came, and a small tremor of betrayal rippled through her. She'd have words with him next time he showed up. If nothing else, she was sure he'd attend his own funeral. And if he didn't show up before then, she'd make sure he was glad he was already dead.

FOURTEEN

The irony of the fact that he could no longer "run for his life" was not wasted on Victor St. John as he ran, leapt, and flew through the darker parts of Seattle. The demons were on his heels, hissing coldly as they always did. He'd seen them as soon as he'd accidentally thrown himself from the helicopter Lacey and… that guy… were in, and the demons had seen him too.

A claw raked across his side, sending a searingly cold sensation through him. He tried dodging around a corner, only to be forcibly reminded of why that no longer worked; three of the dark spirits burst through the wall next to him, surrounding him instantly. Throwing himself toward the sky, he grimaced as their attacks on his mind dragged him toward dark places.

"Rao? Tibbits? Cat? Hey! Why you gotta leave me again?" The cat didn't answer, and he had the sinking feeling that she probably wouldn't save him any sooner than the last second, as she had during his first encounter with Legion in Tokyo. That meant that his only hope was finding a sanctuary in time. The only problem was, he didn't know this part of Seattle— he'd always avoided it in life—and he didn't have the time to pick random strangers' brains on the off chance that they might just happen to be thinking about how to reach the nearest church.

Twisting and turning through the city streets, Victor tried desperately to recall what Rao had taught him about warding demons. He knew, from Rao, they couldn't stand much light, and that they couldn't stand truth. But what did *that* mean? He'd tried quoting facts at them—heck, he'd quoted scriptures and Catholic catechisms—but his efforts hadn't even phased the creatures. And light, well, nothing in nighttime Seattle could glow like Rao had when she'd first saved him and, in fact, the spirits seemed quite comfortable with neon lighting, if the number of demons he'd seen hanging around bars was any indication. All he could do was keep forcing himself forward through his growing despair and desire to curl up into a ball and cease to exist. He felt himself slowing down, felt Legion beginning to surge around him.

Then he thought of Lacey, and the fact that she was now alone with her boss and his thoughts. Summoning all his willpower, he hurled one of the creatures off him, and then another. They bounced back immediately, but in the few seconds he bought, he leapt over a building and happened to spy something that warmed him; a crucifix atop an older structure nearby, with the words "St. Ignatius" on a stone tablet sign on the lawn. He smiled. "Bingo."

The monsters must have seen it too, because they redoubled their efforts to reach him before he could slip through the door, but Victor managed to outrun them. The few that flew into the church behind him pulled up short, and seemed to effervesce in the presence of so many holy symbols and, his gut told him, in the confines of sacred ground. Immediately, they fled, leaving him with time to think.

Too close, he thought. *Every time, too close. I need to figure out how Rao protects herself.*

He took a moment to look around the church. The demons would give up and go away eventually. He hoped they didn't stick around until daybreak like they had that night he holed up in an open-air Japanese shrine just ahead of flying home to America, but he figured he had at least a while before they gave up and went after some other poor, unsuspecting soul. Surveying the room, he found it was like any other Christian church he'd been in; high ceiling, a little stained glass against the wall behind the pulpit on either side of the large cross. Rows of empty pews rested quietly in the dark, but he saw everything perfectly clear. His mind went back to Lacey and he wished she were here with him, instead of trapped with her creepy boss. Out of habit, and real concern for the woman he loved, he dropped to his knees and looked upward.

"So, God, I know I haven't followed Rao's advice to come home. Please don't take that personally. It's not that I *don't* want to go to Heaven. I've always wanted to. But, well, I love her, Lord. And I really want to figure a few things out before I come back. If you'd let me give her a hand for a while, I promise I'll come home once things wrap up. And since I'm trapped in here, and she's still out with that TV guy, could you send her a hand on my behalf? Just get her away from him safely. Amen."

A comforting warmth filled him, and the room seemed to lighten. He glanced around for Rao, but found the sensation of light and heat was general. He looked up again. "Thanks, Lord. That's really cool of you."

Just then, the light from a back office caught Victor's eyes. Curious, he drifted toward it and found the illumination coming from under a backroom door. A voice murmured inside, and Victor leaned in to listen, before realizing that nothing was stopping him from simply walking in; and so he did.

The room was simply furnished; a basic desk and chair set against the wall opposite the door, with only a small, curtained window to provide the occupants with any glimpse of the outside; the drapes were not only drawn, but taped to the wall by the hem. An average-looking computer squatted on the desk next to an old-fashioned corded phone. The handset was pressed up against the ear of a man with an atoll of dark hair surrounding the gleaming bay of his scalp. His face was mousey, and his manners were equally jittery—as though he expected to have to scurry to safety at any given moment. Victor thought, for a moment, about trying to connect with the man's mind and screaming "BOO!" but decided against it at the last moment. Instead, he seated himself on the man's desk, ready to listen in on what may or may not be an amusing conversation.

Mouse-faced man went silent, just then, but Victor could hear the muffled voice coming through the headset; the man on the other end was *clearly* not pleased, and was blaming Victor's unwitting host for whatever problem he was upset about. Curious, Victor calmed his mind the way Rao had taught him, and tuned into the man clutching the handset. Unsurprisingly, all Victor could read from the man was, *I'm so dead. I'm so dead. He's going to murder me and my family and my pets. I'm so dead.*

Victor pulled out of the swirling fear and mental paralysis, and focused on listening to the other man. He caught something about "I expect results by the time I arrive," before the line cut off with an abrupt and violent click. The voice sounded very familiar to Victor, but the poor call quality made it difficult to place perfectly. He sighed, wishing he'd been able to catch more of the unfolding drama. Still curious, he sat and watched as the balding man sagged back in his chair with a shuddering sigh. His surface thoughts were still clear, even without Victor trying to read them, and sweat ran down the little man's face. Abruptly, he sat up and turned on the computer.

When the machine finished booting up, the man in the chair brought up some accounting spreadsheets—clearly ledgers—and began frantically searching them. Victor found that another perk to being dead was that he was able to read and process information considerably faster than in life. Despite the rapid-fire switch between ledgers he managed to gather that the data concerned a number of foreign and domestic transactions. When the words, "Kyoto Consulting" flashed on the screen, Victor sat up at once. The page was gone almost before Victor could think, but in that brief instant, he saw tens of millions of Yens' worth in transactions, and something about "parakeets."

"Wait," Victor said, leaning forward and pointing at the computer, "go back to that last page." The man hesitated for the briefest of moments, a halting look of concern flickering in his eyes, then he went on to another page without so much as glancing in Victor's direction.

"Great. Thanks, dude." Victor stood, and continued to watch the transactions for several minutes, his host frantically alternating between entering data in blank cells and altering monetary figures in others.

"Whoa," Victor said, comprehension dawning, "you're cooking these books *good*." He found the practice despicable, but had to give the little man props for being so skilled; had the guy actually been honest, he could have made a very good accountant from the looks of it.

"So what's a shady dude like you doing in a church office?" Victor wondered aloud. As if in answer to his question, the squeal of brakes sounded outside, followed by a motor cutting out, and a car door slamming a half second later. Mouse-man leapt to his feet, frantically saving his work over and over, as if his very life were about to be erased by a freak computer glitch, and then hurried out of the small office and toward the front door of the church, Victor trailing him. Before the man could reach the vestibule, the front door was thrust open, but caught before it could crash against the wall. A pair of toughs in black clothing and body armor swooped into the room, each one catching one of Mouse-man's arms. A few seconds later, a stately figure in a tailored suit strode through the open door. Victor's eyes went wide.

"Mister Taniguchi?"

His one-time boss made no acknowledgement of Victor's existence, but instead stepped toward the balding man now cowering and squirming in the grasp of the intruders. "Well?" Taniguchi asked Mouse-man.

"I-it's right in there, Mister Taniguchi, sir. All of it. I was just reviewing the data for accuracy moments ago."

Taniguchi arched a brow, and even without mind reading, Victor could tell the man was incredulous. "Very well, Mister Howell. Please show me the data."

"O-of course, Mister Taniguchi, sir. Right this way." With that, the thugs released the small accountant, who then scampered toward the office he had just come from, Taniguchi and his men close behind.

Inside the office, Mouse-man—*No*, Victor thought, *Howell*—quickly took a seat and gestured at the spreadsheet with great animation, like a child showing a pre-school work of art to his parent. "You see, Mister Taniguchi, here are the annual *and* detailed quarterly reports for your entire importing arm. The computing power was abysmal since I had to keep things off the grid, and on one old PC, but I've modified the format to make it more accessible for board meetings. I'm sorry I didn't email it to you; I wasn't expecting you to visit again so soon. I know there is no excuse for my delinquency, but—"

"Sloppy," Taniguchi said quietly leaning forward and peering at the screen. "With the barest glance I can ascertain that you've fabricated these numbers." He straightened, and stared down at his subordinate over his glasses.

"I-I—" Howell stammered, shrinking into his chair as if to escape.

"Now, Mister Howell," Taniguchi said patiently, kneeling next to the terrified man and placing a hand on his trembling shoulder, "I bear the burden of leadership for a vast number of people. This means that I also bear the blame for their mistakes. Are you familiar with the criminal penalties associated with the level of fraud you have just perpetrated?"

Howell shook his head, still clearly terrified. "Not as well as y-you do, sir."

"Then you likely do not know the penalties for fraud in my country."

"Again, n-no, sir."

"Mister Howell," the businessman said, rising, "you are an

113

intelligent man. Intelligent enough to attempt to deceive others by using a Christian church to cover these games you are playing. But I have found you out."

"Sir, I—"

"So I am certain that you understand that if I allow this problem to go unresolved, that I, as the head of my firms, will face trouble on *both* sides of the Pacific. Am I correct?"

Howell merely whimpered and bit his lip.

Taniguchi raised his chin, still eyeing his subordinate. "I cannot allow that to happen. You will correct this problem."

Howell nodded frantically, tears streaming from his eyes.

Taniguchi knelt again and locked eyes with the rodent-like accountant. "And do you know what the problem is?" His subordinate seemed torn between nodding or shaking his head. Victor could sense that the man had already wet his pants. "The problem," Taniguchi said, voice still, but unmistakably clear, "is not the falsification. It's that it is so apparently *obvious* that it can't possibly be missed." Victor felt a pulse of embarrassment at the statement; he'd actually been fooled by the fraud.

"You did not understand the full objective," Taniguchi continued. "You merely made the numbers look pleasing; that is only half of the need."

With that, he stood and abruptly whirled toward the door. He paused at the threshold and, without glancing back, added, "The corrected and impeccable report will be on my desk by sunrise. If I detect so much as a Yen out of place, I will see to it that liability is… appropriately assigned." Then he calmly walked back out the way he came.

Victor followed his ex-boss easily, stunned at what he had just seen. Eager to determine what was going on, Victor fixated on his boss, and looked for a way to merge into his thoughts, and was surprised to find that his surface thoughts were surprisingly still and focused, and revealed nothing of any particular concern. When he tried to press deeper, he felt a strong and active resistance. Taniguchi pulled to a halt at once, and slowly turned in place, piercing eyes searching the dark bowels of the church. Both of his men drew their guns. Victor held perfectly still, somehow wondering whether the man might actually be able to see him. Taniguchi's gaze drifted toward Victor, and stopped. Victor half expected to hear his boss call to him, but instead, Taniguchi's gaze swept onward again. After another few moments, he scowled and turned for the door.

"What was that, boss?" one of the men asked. "Need me to off the nerd?"

Taniguchi waved it away wordlessly and strode out into the night, his men in tow. Victor made to follow him, but didn't make it more than a few feet from the front door before the swarm of darkness ambushed him, driving him back into the vestibule of the church. A light rain began, drawing a curtain of misty blackness over the retreating form of Akio Taniguchi, a man for whom Victor had just lost a mountain of respect.

FIFTEEN

At Victor's closed casket service, New Life Church was nearly filled to capacity. Lacey sat in the 2nd pew behind his closest family, waiting for the procession to start.

She recognized his mother, Karen, surprisingly in all white, even to the hat. She was a petite woman with ethereal blond hair, dabbing her puffy eyes. Victor's father bore a clear resemblance to him, with broad shoulders and thick dark hair, one arm embracing his weeping wife, while he, too, openly shed tears.

Victor took a seat beside Lacey, glumly waiting. He felt deep sorrow for his parents' loss, wishing he could pat a hand on their shoulders and tell them everything was alright, that he indeed was still alive, just on to the next phase of *life*.

For a moment he entered his mother's thoughts. The grief was too strong for him to bear. A web of confusion, of unanswered questions, engulfed him. *He's too young* was echoed over and over by the word "*Why?*" He yanked himself out, and shook his head in his hands.

It will be okay, Lacey said, touching what appeared to others to be the empty space beside her. Although she couldn't feel him, she could still see him. *Even if I wanted to kill you for abandoning me the other night.*

Victor turned his head to her. "Hey, I wasn't abandon—"

She hushed him with a thought, and he sensed that she understood his predicament without him saying it. Her eyes were red, a single teardrop gliding down her smooth cheek. "You really miss me, don't you?" he said.

The corner of Lacey's red-lipsticked lips turned up ever-so-slightly. Although she was staring straight ahead, at crosses adorning his black casket, she mentally spoke directly to him. *You are a dear person in my life, Victor St. John. I will treasure every moment we have left together.*

He smirked. "You're just happy to find out you won't be reincarnated into a cockroach."

She rolled her eyes. *Oh, please. Actually, you dashed my dreams of someday becoming Queen of England.*

He laughed at that. "Hey—when we're done with the service, we need to talk about the other night. You know, you and your boss? Oh, and I found some things that might interest you."

Lacey didn't hide her frown. *I'd rather not remember that night*, she thought. *But*, and she sighed, *I think we need to discuss it nonetheless.*

"I said a prayer for you, you know," Victor said. "Last night, at another church. Looks like it worked. You're okay."

Lacey actually felt a little tug at her heart to hear that, but she didn't let it through, instead keeping her eyes fixed on the preacher who stood to start the service by appropriately reading passages from The Bible on "the love of God." Lacey found the sentiment sweet, despite her theological differences.

There was a subtle squeak of a large door opening from the right rear of the chapel. Victor automatically turned to see who would be his last guest. Surprisingly, it was Taniguchi. The Asian man took a remaining space closest to the exit.

Taniguchi patted and smoothed his tie, keeping a straight face. Victor growled. "*Lacey*," he hissed. "Don't turn around, but my old boss is here. I'll tell you about it later, but I found out some… really not cool things about him last night."

Please be quiet, Victor. Lacey's thoughts returned. *I'm in the middle of mourning your death. This service is very touching. You really should pay attention—it won't happen again.*

Victor grimaced slightly. "Fine." And yet, he was more interested in seeing who had come to memorialize him than he was in what was being said about him.

As he scanned the room, he spotted someone else he knew all too well, sitting rather alone, as there was space to the left and right of her. Jessica wore a black cocktail dress with glitter across the bust. He knew she liked large sunglasses, but today hers were huge, perched just under a wavy black sunhat. One would think she was trying to go incognito with such accessories. Victor's sight automatically zoomed in on her eyes; through the dark glasses, he saw tears brimming.

"My boss and Jessica are both here," Victor quietly told Lacey.

Lacey didn't turn to see, not wanting to be obvious. Perhaps she would approach them at the close of the service. Those were the only two guests of the funeral who she knew had connections to Victor's time in Japan. She crossed her legs, the skirt of her simple black dress grazing her knees.

It was a beautiful occasion. An hour later, after the closing prayer, Lacey stood, and scanned the room. Victor pointed out where Jessica and Taniguchi were seated. She thought she should at least speak to his former boss. Upon exiting the pew, however, Victor's mother grabbed Lacey's shoulder.

"I have something to give you," she said with a smile through tears.

"Okay." Lacey glanced back at Taniguchi, who was already out the door. With so many people swarming the aisles to leave, she realized she wouldn't have a chance to catch him, anyhow.

"Let's go somewhere more private," the woman said. Linking arms with Lacey, she ushered her through a side door, and down a dark end of the hall. No one was around.

Karen affectionately took hold of Lacey's hands. She paused, taking in a deep breath, nervousness apparent. Through tears she gave a giggle. "I'm so happy you could be here."

Lacey just sympathetically nodded, and gave Karen a hug.

After the warm embrace, Karen unzipped her pastel pink purse. She said, her fingers shaking, "As you know, Paul and I went to Japan to pick up Victor's things… and arrange with the authorities to fly his body home."

"Yes?"

"The police met with us. Anyway, they had retrieved something from Victor's pocket." She pinched around the purse some more. "They wanted to make sure it was in our possession before leaving."

"Okay," Lacey said on the edge of her metaphorical seat. "And this is something you want to give *me*?"

"Well…" Karen took her hand out, trying to form the right words. "It was something Victor wanted to give you. He really loved you, and I just want to say you would have made a beautiful daughter-in-law." She wiped some tears.

Karen plucked a small black velvet box out of her purse.

Perplexed, Lacey narrowed her eyes at it. "Uh…" She almost stopped her, knowing she had already found the engagement ring.

The woman opened the box to reveal a simple round diamond on a white gold band.

Dumbfounded, Lacey said, "You're sure this is for me?" She shifted her eyes all around, looking for Victor in vain.

Karen vigorously nodded, her hat shaking atop her thin hair. "You were the girl who captured his heart. He had called me the morning of his… passing… and told me of his plan to present you with an engagement ring."

Hesitantly, Lacey accepted the gift in the palm of her hand. "I'm sorry, I'm just speechless," she said for reasons other than Karen could know.

"It's okay. It can be hard to take it all in. I understand." She rubbed Lacey's arm.

Without thinking, Lacey said aloud, "I need to talk to him."

Victor's mother sputtered back a sob. "Yes, I wish I could

talk to him too."

Lacey gave another warm embrace. "Thank you so much for this. I will cherish it forever."

Victor! Lacey yelled in her mind. *We need to talk!*

*

The luncheon afterward at Victor's parents' was hard to deal with. Lacey wanted to find out who owned the ring she had found in the ash. It would be a major clue as to who was Victor's murderer. Victor had answered Lacey's summons after only a brief delay, excusing himself with a remark about his dead pet cat. Lacey had ignored it, and told him they'd speak at the luncheon. And now, here they were, Lacey seated at the kitchen island in the St. John home amid the murmur of the other guests, while Victor floated in front of her in a meditative stance.

When Lacey carefully opened the ring box for Victor to see, he gave a low whistle. "I can't believe you thought I could afford a gigantic marquis diamond, anyway, and on a platinum band, no less." Victor shook his head, eyeing the hors d'oeuvres with a gleam of craving in his blue eyes. "Mom made her best chicken salad and I can't even smell it. Sometimes I really hate being dead."

Lacey bit into a carrot dipped in ranch and mentally retorted, *Marquis are my favorite!*

"Does that mean I could afford one any easier?" He chuckled.

You're right. You were a student intern. I should have known, except logic kinda flies out the window when your ex-boyfriend is suddenly dead.

He sobered quickly. "I would have found a way to do it for you, Lacey. You were worth it."

Lacey felt herself flush.

Victor shifted out of his stance and drifted to the floor, quirking his back to look like he was actually leaning against the kitchen's island. "I should tell you now, before you get more disappointed down the road—the diamond isn't real. It was a placeholder for the real thing that I could afford later."

A cubic zirconium? She lifted her brows.

A gentle hand on Lacey's shoulder took her out of her discussion with Victor. It was Deborah McMahon of all people. Even at a funeral, the woman managed to look absolutely perky, smiling brightly with pink lipstick.

"Hi!" she said, giving Lacey a stiff, tight hug. "How're you holding up?" She pulled back. Her coiffed brunette hair stayed in perfect position, curled at the shoulders.

"Deborah… I didn't expect you to be here," Lacey said, and added apologetically, "I mean, hello! I'm holding up. I'm sorry, did you know Victor?"

"Goodness, no." She shook her head. "I can't imagine how you must be feeling right now. No, I heard the news from Greg last night that you quit. He told me the shock over what transpired with your ex was too much to bear. Since we've been coworkers over the last almost five years, I thought it would only be the right thing for me to swing by and give my condolences, you know?"

"Oh, well, thank you very much."

Deborah asked, her face more serious, "What are your plans now? Where will you go? What will you do?"

"I'm going to stay in the area, and take some time figuring that out."

"So you're staying at the same apartment?"

Lacey nodded.

"Good to know, in case I want to bring over a tub of ice cream for comfort." She smiled so big, her green eyes looked tight. "Hey, I won't take any more of your time up. I just wanted to stop by."

Upon the woman exiting the kitchen, Victor said, "Who was that, and how many uppers is she on? I tried reading her mind and it was like a nuclear blast of *chipper*."

Lacey hurried out the kitchen's back door and went directly to her car, Victor trailing behind.

"What are you doing?" he asked.

"I need to visit Jenning's Jewelers," she said out loud,

nobody in earshot.

"If you want to return the ring I got you, that's fine, but I didn't get it from Jenning's. I got it from Walmart."

Lacey whipped open her car door and halted. "*Walmart?*" she sneered.

Victor shrugged a shoulder. "What?"

"It's getting worse by the second. The next thing you'll tell me is you stole it off a homeless woman standing outside the automotive department."

"No, it was ordered online. Walmart shipped it from the States." That earned him a glare. He got the picture. "I should just... zip my lips."

Lacey cracked a smile. "Anyway, I'm going to Jenning's because their logo was on the ring's box I found at your place. Maybe they can help. It's a good clue."

"I'll go with you," he said, promptly.

SIXTEEN

Jenning's Jewelers was a quaint store, sharing a parking lot with a dry cleaners. Its locale was easy enough for Lacey to remember, however, as KZTB's towering headquarters gleamed in the gray sky just two blocks down. She had once accidentally entered the jewelry store, intending to pick up her white, silk blouse. If it weren't for the need to track down clues to Victor's murder, Lacey never would have, even accidentally, stepped foot in there again. The owner apparently liked antiques and owls, or rather antique owls, as they sat at various heights, perched in the darndest places. All the eyes were a bit unsettling.

Showing the jeweler the box, and its accompanying dazzler, Lacey said, "This was lost and found. I'm trying to return it to its rightful owner."

The older woman peered through tiny glasses, hooked to a chain necklace, and tottering atop a beakish nose. "Mm-hm, I remember this ring. It was sold to a very handsome gentleman."

"Go on."

"He said the special woman in mind wouldn't expect it in the least bit. Best part was, for me, he paid in *cash*. Twenty-two *thousand* dollars."

"That's a great memory you have there." Lacey tucked some hair behind an ear. "Do you have a name, a description of the man?"

"Oh, I don't need a great memory for that," she said. "All of our jewelry sales are on file with the buyer's name, address, everything, not only for insurance purposes, but because of our best warranty in Seattle. All our customers have a warranty that promises to replace any lost or damaged gemstones as long as they bring their jewelry to the store for a quarterly cleaning."

Lacey leaned in. "Great, so you'll tell me?"

"Heavens no. That information is all strictly confidential. It's our policy." She shook a long finger in chastisement.

Great! Lacey thought. *The ol' bat isn't going to budge.*

"Play hardball with her," Victor said. "Tell her you'll just have to keep the ring and sell it on Ebay or something for a pretty penny."

Lacey placed a hand over the jewelry box, saying, "And what's the policy for 'Finders Keepers'?"

The woman said, stepping back, "I'm sorry, I don't follow…"

Lacey swiped up the ring and stuffed it into her purse. "That's because there is no such thing as a Finders Keepers policy. I could sell it on Ebay and get another, matching tennis bracelet." She longingly eyed the glittering jewelry around her dainty wrist.

Obviously annoyed, the jeweler said, "Why don't you leave it up to me? I'll contact the buyer myself, and tell them to come down here to pick it up."

Lacey retorted, "I'm not leaving a ring here without any assurances that it will in fact get back to the rightful owner. For all I know, the ring could have just been placed in this box, and come from Walmart."

The woman sneered, a hand over her heart. "Walmart?"

Victor groaned. "I'm never going to live this one down, am I?"

"I need proof somehow," Lacey said.

"Our store has an A rating with The Better Business Bureau."

"Look, you're not understanding." Lacey's eyes widened. "I need to see with my own two eyes that this gets returned to the right person. I'm certain the owner won't care one iota that you broke some sort of confidentiality policy, as long as their precious engagement ring is back in their hands."

The woman huffed, her spectacles shaking in frustration. "Fine. I think there's something that may satisfy you."

She trundled to a back room, and was heard opening a drawer of files, and flipping through them. Victor teleported, hovering over her hunched shoulder. The woman pulled out a green file and licked a thick thumb, before resuming.

This lady does things Old School, Victor thought, eyeing the folder. He'd have put all that information in a spreadsheet. Still this close to finding what might be a good lead... if he had a beating heart, it would've been racing in anticipation. Who *else's* engagement ring was found in his apartment the night he was killed?

"Aha," she muttered under her breath, pulling out one contract/receipt in particular. She quickly made a copy of it from a dinosaur machine in the corner, occupying about half the room.

Victor followed her, trying to catch the customer name, and finally got a good view of it as the copy came off the machine: John Smith. Who the heck was John Smith? The jeweler used a black Sharpie to black out the name on the copy.

Coming with the copy smugly in hand, the woman returned to Lacey at the counter. She placed it on the glass top, and said, "Here is the proof." On the sheet was a black and white picture of the ring, with its exact cut, color, and quality listed beside it. No wonder it was a huge diamond—it said it was two whole carats. At the top of the form, the customer's name was blacked out.

Victor appeared next to Lacey. "The name was John Smith."

Good job! Lacey, happy he caught that, pulled the ring back out of her purse. She said to the jeweler, "Do you mind calling Jo—? Him?" She caught herself.

"No problem at all," she said with a fake smile. She pulled a rotary phone with a curly cord out from under a nearby cash register. She dialed. Victor flashed beside her to listen in, cheek-to-cheek, like he'd done with Jessica. The response was easily heard: an operator's voice robotically announced that the number had been disconnected or was no longer in service.

Instead of hanging up, the lady oddly said, "Good afternoon, this is Jenning's Jewelry calling... Yes, hello... Well, I'm calling because someone turned in the engagement ring you purchased, saying they found it... Wonderful! We'll look forward to you coming by to claim your lost ring today, then. Thank you again for choosing us." She put down the receiver with a smile.

Victor blurted, "Don't give her the ring!"

"Why not?" Lacey blurted back.

"Pardon me?" the jeweler responded, as Victor watched a black being start to seep out of the old telephone. He backed quickly away; he'd never seen Legion during daylight. But the thing was sluggish, and didn't seem to take notice of him, thankfully.

"Sorry, I was speaking to... never mind." Lacey's voice drooped.

"The number was disconnected," Victor said, urging, "Just get out of here. Now!"

Lacey's heart suddenly squeezed by fear, she rushed out the front door.

"Hey! *Wait!*" the woman barked, nearly leaping over the counter.

Quickly behind her Lincoln's wheel, Lacey peeled out of the small parking lot. Victor beside her, she trembled. "That lady suddenly gave me the creeps."

"That's because she had evil intents," he said matter-of-factly.

Lacey kind of glanced at him, her grip on the steering wheel still tight. "Thank you for listening in on her call. Now that you're kind of on the 'other side,' do you read people's auras… or whatever they're called?"

"No. It's not like that. But I do see things." He didn't feel like divulging the horrifying details of Legion to her. *It's already bad enough that mortals know evil exists*, he thought to himself. *She doesn't need to know its face, or lack thereof.*

That gave Lacey a chill. "At least we got the name of the murderer. Who's John Smith?"

"Heck if I know." He put his arms up.

Lacey's brow wrinkled. "You don't know?"

"Nope."

"You don't think, do you, that the ring could have belonged to one of the emergency personnel—a firefighter? EMT?" She put her sunglasses on, and eased her grip, heading downtown, toward her apartment. She suddenly felt the need to check on Nainai.

"Trust me, none of them would have a white bread name like John Smith. And why would a Japanese cop or firefighter purchase a ring from Seattle?"

Lacey nodded. "Of course. I'm just still a bit shaken up. He's an American, white."

Victor joked, "…Has wavy blond hair, a square jawline and can sing a duet to *Colors of the Wind.*"

"Ha ha." Lacey laughed sarcastically. "We can check the phone book, when we get to my place."

"You have a phone book? Do those still exist?"

"Of course, it's where I get all my handy plumber and dentist magnets for my refrigerator."

Victor paused.

"I'm kidding."

Victor rolled his eyes. "Hey, so I wanted to talk to you about some stuff I found out last night. Remember my boss from this summer's internship?"

Lacey nodded. "You practically worshipped the guy. It was really nice of him to come to your funeral. I wouldn't expect that of someone as powerful as he is."

"He's committing corporate fraud, Lacey."

She frowned. "Wait, how did you get from 'Mister Taniguchi is my hero' to 'Mister Taniguchi is a criminal'?"

Victor leaned forward and rested his head in a hand, a gesture that looked as natural in death as it had in life. "I spent last night at St. Ignatius."

"The Catholic church not far from here?"

"That's the one. It seems churches and other holy sites are my best bet for a stress-free night."

Lacey quirked an eyebrow.

"Let's just say there are really bad... things... that come out at night." Even the memory made him shudder. "Anyway, Taniguchi showed up there last night."

"I thought he was Zen Buddhist." Lacey stopped at a red light, and turned to look at Victor. For just a moment, she forgot he was dead, and was stunned at just how handsome he was, and about how nice a guy he was. Had things only been just a little bit different...

Victor smiled. "I heard that. And Lacey—I do love you."

Lacey blushed and cleared her throat, facing forward again and begging the light to change.

"Anyway, Taniguchi met up with some half-price crook of an accountant, there. The guy was using a church as his hideout while he cooked Taniguchi's books."

Lacey frowned. "So what does that have to do with your death? Are you saying your old boss arranged to have you killed?"

Victor shook his head. "I don't think so; I never found anything that struck me as incriminating. I was just really shocked and figured I'd tell you. But wow—seeing those ledgers? That man has his finger in *everything*. I mean, he even exports parakeets, of all things."

Lacey hit the brakes reflexively, and a car behind her screeched to a stop, horn blaring. She hid her blush, and pulled to the curb as she waved the other driver by. She ignored the choice words and flashing finger. "Did you say 'parakeets'?"

Victor nodded. "Yeah. Why?"

"Remember what I told you at the Space Needle about parakeets? You never asked me about my night with Greg."

Victor felt a simmering rage, then deflated, realizing that he'd been so caught up in himself that he *hadn't* stopped to see how Lacey had fared; at least he'd had the good sense to pray for her. "Okay. So how was your night with… him?"

Lacey rolled her eyes and swatted at Victor out of habit. "Don't be such a baby. I've *never* had any feelings for Greg Mendoza, aside from professional interest. Even if he *weren't* married, he's not my type."

"I get the picture," Victor said stiffly. He hated the thought of *his* girl alone with another man. "Just get on with it."

"Such a gentleman," Lacey cooed mockingly. "As I was saying, Greg showed me his warehouse. Tried to buy me back by offering me a raise, a promotion, and a cut of his export business."

Victor perked up. "Did you say—?"

"Yes. Export. Just like I said back at the Space Needle. I knew he wasn't being upfront with me."

Victor's brow furrowed. "So were you right about the exporting?"

Lacey grimaced. "Somewhat. Mostly aphrodisiacs and cosmetics," and she blanked her mind against the memory of what had almost happened with Greg, "and the warehouse had a huge room full of caged parakeets; those were imports, not exports. And there were crates with children's pictures on them."

Victor gestured for her to continue. "Meaning?"

Lacey narrowed her eyes. "Meaning I don't know. I *think* Greg might be into child trafficking, but I have no proof at all."

"And you're saying that my old boss does business with your old boss. So what does *that* mean? That they're both crooked?"

Lacey shrugged, checked traffic for an opening, and pulled

back on to the street to continue home. "I don't know *what* it means, my dear Victor. I only know that Greg works with some… Watanabe guy and—"

"Wait—Orochi Watanabe?"

Lacey nodded.

Victor pursed his lips. "I think that seals it. Mister Watanabe is half-partner, half-rival with Mister Taniguchi. They did business together in Tokyo. It makes sense they'd work together on other things. But aside from them being shady, is this even worth our time? Ms. Tibbitts—Rao, whatever—might find some way to drag me back to Heaven at any minute. I can't waste my time playing crime fighter. I stayed to find out who killed me." He paused, then added, softly, "But I mostly stayed for you."

Lacey wasn't sure she managed to completely hide her blush, but she kept it from her voice when she answered. "That's very sweet, Victor." An idea struck her at random. "Wait—you said you saw Taniguchi meet with an accountant at the church?"

Victor nodded. "Yeah. Why?"

"Wasn't that what *you* were doing for him? Accounting?"

Victor nodded again, slowly. "Are you saying…?"

Lacey glanced at him. "Maybe you came a little too close to finding something out after all."

He shuddered, then sat back in his seat to think. "Maybe I did. Before last night, I would have said you were crazy to think that Mister Taniguchi would do something like that. But the way that other guy acted even when he was just on the phone with my boss? I'm not so sure I'd put it past the guy now. I wonder how close I was to finding out about his fraud." A chilling thought brushed Victor's mind. "Wait—you said you thought your ex-boss might have been involved in child trafficking, right?"

Lacey's beautiful face soured. "I hope I'm *not* right."

Victor ground his teeth. "Maybe I was about to find about *that* too. I need to visit that warehouse. Can we turn around?"

She shook her head. "I've been away from Nainai too long.

She has trouble even feeding herself, let alone taking care of personal hygiene. Maybe tomorrow. I get really nervous whenever I leave her alone."

Victor nodded. "It'll wait. Let's get back and help Grandma. We can sleep on everything else."

*

Lacey soon entered her dark apartment, Victor in tow. "Nainai? I'm home?" There was no response. Only the murmur of a television soap opera, complete with dramatic music, broke the eerie silence.

"Nainai?" Lacey stepped out of the foyer and around the corner into her living room, and was greeted by the sight of an empty hideaway bed; Nainai *never* left her plush couch-bed without Lacey's help. An unwelcome chill ran down her spine.

SEVENTEEN

"Nainai! Nainai, where are you?"

A crash and the clatter of broken glass came from the master bedroom. Lacey dropped her purse and sprinted toward the sound, visions of someone kicking in her window swirling in her mind. "*Nainai*!"

Lacey skidded to a halt just inside the bedroom door. Rather than an intruder, she saw her grandmother sitting in her wheelchair, her head in her hands. Down on the wood floor, close by, were white shards.

Lacey exhaled in relief.

"I'm sorry," Nainai said. "I'm so sorry."

"What are you doing in here?" Lacey asked, kneeling beside her sympathetically. She spotted what remained of a ceramic paw.

"I was bored... and scared," she said. Her wrinkled fingers now spread over her cheeks. "I felt a... presence. There was some creaking near the kitchen. So I was trying to get my good luck cat. I wanted it in the living room with me."

Lacey wiped her grandmother's hair as she drew her against her chest for a soothing hug. "It's okay. Everything is okay."

"No." Nainai pulled back, looking Lacey in the eyes, her

eyelids puffy. "I broke my feng shui cat, and so now we won't have good luck. A curse will fall upon your place, and it's my doing."

"I don't believe in curses." At least Lacey didn't *think* she did. Why hadn't that eerie feeling totally left? "Everything will be fine, especially now that I've resigned from my job—"

"You quit your *job*?" Nainai protested. "How will you afford this place? Ancestors, help us!" She cupped her hands together. "The curse has already started."

"No, no curse has started!" She placed both hands on Nainai's shoulders. "I don't want to hear any more of this. Look, I will get you a new cat. It will be even luckier than the old one."

Nainai actually looked a bit relieved. "It has to be bigger. Big!"

"In the words of Donald Trump, it will be *huge*."

"I'm so sorry…"

"I'm the one who's sorry, Nainai. You told me you wanted your cat in the living room with you, and I got distracted. But everything will be okay. I promise. We can have the rest of the day together. Tonight, I'll look online and buy rush order shipping on a cat."

Did somebody say cat? Rao popped beside Victor, who was watching quietly from the doorway.

"Only about a million times," Victor said. "Where have you been? I have a ton of questions for you."

Will you look at the time? Rao said. *I guess I should be going.*

*

Later that evening, Victor had gone to New Life Church to spend an uneventful night there. He'd apologized that he couldn't keep watch over Lacey's place, but he still hadn't figured out how to fight whatever evil spirits he claimed to see, and added a remark about how his pet cat wasn't forthcoming on teaching him self-defense against the dark arts. Lacey had retorted with a Harry Potter comment, but she could tell Victor was sincere in his desires to not abandon her. Still, shortly before sunset, he slipped through her front wall, disappearing with a promise of being back at first light, leaving Lacey to follow up the lead on the jewelry.

Unfortunately, she had no success in reaching any John Smith who knew anything to do with an engagement ring. Lacey started to wonder if it were perhaps a John or Jane Doe purchase, to remain anonymous. The jeweler had mentioned the buyer paid in cash. After another fruitless phone call, the doorbell rang. Annoyed by the interruption, but grateful for the short break, she wrapped her sweater tighter around her waist, and approached the door in white slippers. Passing Nainai in the living room bed, she was stopped with a, "Don't answer that. Who comes this late?"

Lacey answered, glancing at her Apple watch. "It's only 8:32." She peeked in the peephole. The shadowed figure on the doorstep was female, Lacey determined, having a smaller frame and hair with plenty of body. She unhooked her chain lock, and opened the door.

It was Deborah. "Hi! Hope it's not too late!" She presented a white bakery box. "This is a cake from us at KZTB, since we never had a proper goodbye ceremony for you, under the circumstances. I called up a few friends, like Cathy and *Greg*, to chip in on this for STAT delivery tonight. It was a group effort, but they weren't able to make it. I'm simply the delivery girl. No tip necessary!" She awkwardly laughed through a stretched smile.

"Oh, wow, that was very thoughtful." Lacey touched her chin, wondering why Cathy hadn't been the one to bring it by. She turned toward the foyer. "Would you like to come in, have a bite with me?"

Deborah said, "Oh, goodness, no. I don't want to take up your evening. But do you think I could use your restroom? I waited thirty minutes in Bliss Bakery, and have to tinkle."

"Sure, no problem. Please, come in." Lacey took the cake gratefully, and pointed her to a restroom down the hall.

While Deborah was doing her business, Lacey set the cake

on the kitchen table. She sat there a moment, still wondering about the ring and its owner. She finally peeled the tape on the edge of the box and was about to lift the lid, but was interrupted by Deborah's chipper voice. "All done!"

She had approached from behind, startling Lacey.

Lacey breathed. "Oh, okay. Thank you again for this."

"My pleasure."

The woman was out the door, the next moment, leaving Lacey alone with the tune of Nainai turning over in bed, readjusting pillows.

Rain started to patter against the apartment, which wasn't unusual, considering their locale. But tonight it came with a foreboding chill. Lacey again wrapped her sweater tighter, and sat back at her kitchen table. Something wasn't right.

"Don't eat the cake," Nainai said nonchalantly.

That was definitely unexpected. "Why not?" Lacey asked.

"Confucious say, 'Never accept treats from druggies.'"

Lacey cocked a brow with disbelief. "What makes you think Deborah's a druggie?"

"She used your bathroom but didn't flush the toilet."

Lacey put her elbows on the table. "What does that have to do with anything?"

"You're the investigative journalist. Do you want to check for a floater? Or see if pills are missing from the medicine cabinet?"

"Hm, that's quite the analysis." Lacey perked up. "Did you happen to see KZTB's nightly special on opioid abuse, warning realtors to lock up medicine during open houses?"

"No, *stupid* is across the globe, baby girl."

Before heading to the bathroom, Lacey deadbolted and chain-locked the front door. KZTB actually aired a nightly special on opioid abuse, wherein they warned realtors of addicts stealing drugs from medicine cabinets.

There was no hint in the toilet bowl of any unflushed business. Lacey knew better, anyway. Deborah was as pristine as she was perky. As far as medicine cabinets go, thankfully Lacey's stash was limited to a trio of pill bottles for Nainai.

One called Aricept, to combat early signs of Dementia. Another was a blood thinner, Warfarin. And lastly, a Chinese herbal supplement that Lacey didn't know much about, as it seemed too much of mystical mumbo-jumbo to care for; she couldn't read the Mandarin words anyway. She unscrewed each lid and counted. Of course everything was fine, because there weren't any mood/pain changers in the lot.

Shaking the bottles beside Nainai, moments later, Lacey said, "If she took anything, it was from the green herbal bottle."

"Figures," her grandmother huffed. "That was my pot."

Lacey arched a brow.

"I'm teasing." She laughed loudly, clapping her hands like a child. "You should have seen your face. That's just vitamins."

"I'm about to buy you a new lucky cat, and that's how you treat me?" she teased back.

Lacey retreated to the kitchen. The rain's pattering became more aggressive, sounding more like buckets of water being thrown against the windows. She filled a teapot with water and put it on the stove in thought. Who killed Victor? Watanabe or Taniguchi, or the two of them in cahoots? But then who was John Smith? Either one of them, she supposed. She suddenly remembered Greg's comment when they'd visited his warehouse on River Street. That *had* been the place she'd covered a money laundering scheme. If she had to guess, she suspected Taniguchi and Watanabe would be laundering their money to cover their tracks; which meant they'd have exorbitant amounts of spare cash to burn, and would be looking for things to buy that weren't easily traceable.

Which one would have purchased the ring? And why would they have had it if they'd gone to Victor's apartment? She wished she could recall Watanabe's death-grip on her upper arm. She tried willing an image of his ring finger. Was it bare? She paused, pulling an herbal mint tea bag out of a box. Perhaps her thoughts were leading her down the wrong path, a rabbit trail. What if it didn't matter whether the murderer was married or single, because maybe the ring wasn't intended for anybody? Maybe it *was* just one of the ways the murderer laundered money.

Lacey lifted the teapot's lid and dipped the minty bag into it, letting its string hang out the edge. While she waited for steam to cause a whistle, she again returned to the table, to her cake. She lifted the box lid, and inside was a small round cake wrapped in hot pink fondant icing. Written in loopy letters, red frosting said, "Farewell, Lacey."

Lacey Ling thought nothing of the message, until the next morning, when she became violently ill.

EIGHTEEN

Clinging to the toilet bowl, Lacey heaved what little bile was left in her pained stomach, before crumpling to the ground in a jerky shiver. She moaned, cold sweat running down her forehead and chest.

She had only had a tiny slice of the cake, but that *had* to be it. If she had a regular slice, would she be dead right now? Thankfully Nainai had refused a piece. Lacey didn't want to think of what could've happened if her grandmother accepted. *Farewell, Lacey*, it read. *Farewell.*

Victor hadn't come over yet. She figured it was eight-something in the morning. Out of being a gentleman, he wouldn't show until at least nine, knowing there was "getting ready" time. Lacey thought of her phone. Should she call an ambulance?

Nainai's voice drifted to her from the living room. "You've been sounding like a barking seal for the last half hour. I told you not to eat the cake!"

Lacey clenched her teeth, feeling her stomach roil more. She moaned again, this time longer. *Why would Deborah do this?* she wondered. *What did I do to deserve this?* It had been out of character for the woman to be so thoughtful of another, but Lacey decided that under the circumstance, Victor's death, maybe things were different. She gave her the benefit of the doubt. She wouldn't be so trusting of someone so selfish ever again, if she lived through this.

A sudden sharp pain, like scissors, knifed through Lacey's back. Shoulder blades reactively rammed together as she howled. The sickness was getting worse by the moment. Where was her phone? By her bed? With every ounce of energy, Lacey pushed herself on to her knees, on all fours, and slogged, like moving through a pool of molasses, into the hall.

"I'm going to get out of bed and help you!" Nainai called again. "You're not even responding in any way coherently! I'm getting really worried!"

No, Lacey thought, but it came out in a lower grunt, a drop of saliva stringing from her loose lips. The wood floor started to wave beneath her, and a halo of blackness was closing in on her vision, until she couldn't see anymore, or feel anymore.

*

Lacey awoke to the feeling of her right arm's blood going cold. She blinked a few times, hearing a beeping in the background. Oh yeah, she was at the hospital, an IV in her arm. She vaguely remembered being put on a stretcher and rolled out into an ambulance, cold rain drizzling down on her and the EMTs.

Victor hovered beside her. "Hey there," he said softly, unmistakably worried.

Lacey said, "I hope you're not here to tell me you're taking me to your God's kingdom. Am I still alive?"

"Yes, you are plenty alive," someone else said before Victor. Lacey flopped her head to her right where a middle-aged man in scrubs had just entered her room. He approached her bedside. "I'm Dr. Spellman." He pulled a light-pen out of his pocket, and looked at her pupils. "How are you feeling?"

She was suddenly brought back to the awareness of her muscles aching, and the pit of her stomach feeling raw. "I've been better." She thought of Nainai. "Where's my grandma?"

"She's here. She came over with you in the ambulance. She's pretty adamant that you were poisoned. What do you think about that?"

Lacey thought of the cake again, and Deborah's smile that, in remembrance, now seemed fake. "That's what I thought, too."

His eyebrows went up a touch. "That's a pretty serious thing to say, unless you're talking about typical food poisoning. We'll take a blood test to see precisely what's going on here, okay? It may just be a flu."

"That would be a pretty bad flu," Lacey said, repositioning her pillow behind tangled hair. Her chills came back, feeling like her sheet and thin blanket were suddenly yanked off her. She moaned. Victor put a hand over hers, and Lacey felt a moment of warmth.

A nurse stepped up beside the doctor and pulled out the implements for a blood draw. Spellman flicked his gaze at Lacey as the nurse dabbed her arm with iodine and began searching for a vein. The look in his eyes made Lacey wonder if things might be worse than she'd thought.

*

As soon as the labs came back, Dr. Spellman entered Lacey's room. He took his stool and scooted close to her. "I have some disconcerting news, but first I'll say that you're in good hands. Everything is going to be fine. What I want to do is ask you a couple questions, since you and your grandmother both shared concerns over a possible poisoning."

Lacey nodded weakly. Victor, at the other side of the bed, listened with anticipation.

"It's actually one of my standard questions, anyway, along with 'Do you smoke?' and 'Are you pregnant?' So, do you take any illegal drugs?"

"No," she said fast.

"Does anyone you associate with do drugs?"

She thought of Deborah, what Nainai said about her being

a druggie. "Well, I have my suspicions but no proof."

"Your test showed positive for opium."

Victor interjected, "Greg. It has to be him!"

"I was thinking Deborah, not Greg," Lacey said out loud.

The doctor, obviously thinking she was talking to him, said, "Who's Deborah?"

"Deborah works with me, or rather did work with me. I recently resigned. She came to my place last night offering a 'Farewell' cake. I ate some of it this morning, and became ill."

"You mentioned a Greg. Who's he?"

"Greg… is my former boss. The last time I was with him was two nights ago, though." Should she tell him what went down, that night in the warehouse? She decided to be subtle about the details, not really wanting cops to come to the hospital… if that's how it worked.

"Did you eat anything he gave you?"

"No…" She thought of the cosmetics. "He did give me two perfume bottles, though. I sprayed some on me that night. Actually, I sprayed quite a bit. The smell was… divine."

Dr. Spellman crossed his arms, a thoughtful look of concern in his eyes. "How did you feel after spraying it?"

Lacey nearly blushed through her sickness. She hated admitting to it, especially with Victor right there. "I remember feeling a soft, happy feeling, kind of warm inside. Everything I touched was perfect."

Her dead ex-boyfriend eyed her with a brow raised.

Victor, please don't dive into my mind right now. I'll spare you the details. We didn't kiss, okay? Victor turned away, but she still felt his frown.

Sketching some notes, the doctor said, "I'd be concerned more about your former employer than your coworker. Your description of the effect of the perfume exactly matches the effects associated with opium. However, in regards to your symptoms this morning—*eating* opium, even deadly amounts, wouldn't leave you sick without at least a temporary high."

Lacey accepted the fact. He was the expert. "I shouldn't have thought of Deborah. Being sick like this can make you have weird thoughts, though…"

"And it's quite possible the drugs in your system may have placed you in an immunocompromised state that left you more susceptible than normal to disease." He shook his head. "Your bloodwork shows you're fighting an infection. We'll need to do more labs to rule out a few more things. Before I do, is there anything else you think I should know? I'm here to help."

She thought of the parakeets, the stench, the dust, their gooey eyes. A dark warehouse was no place to pack birds. They looked sick. She'd heard of bird flus; could it be? She divulged. The physician nodded thoughtfully, and said he'd consider avian-borne illnesses in his research. With a few notes, he bid Lacey farewell, and left.

*

Results came back sooner than expected. Lacey was on her second IV bag, with a medicine drip of some kind, her lungs feeling a bit weak. Dr. Spellman gave her the news that she indeed had contracted an infection from birds: Psittacosis, or in layman terms, Parrot Fever.

"We're going to give you Doxycycline, an antibiotic. You should start feeling better in forty-eight hours."

"Is that when I'll be discharged?"

"Yes," Dr. Spellman said, smiling, "you should be well enough to return home by then."

Lacey grimaced. "I can't leave my grandmother alone that long. Where will she go?"

The older man nodded thoughtfully. "We'll arrange care with a nursing home, unless you have any emergency contacts you'd prefer to use."

Lacey sighed. "My parents live in Oklahoma." She thought of people from KZTB. It was hard to trust mere coworkers or acquaintances, at such a time, and she didn't want to impose on Cathy, either. Too weak and exhausted to feel anger rise within, however, her head flopped to the left, against her pillow, toward Victor. He had a look of fiery revenge in his translucent blue eyes. "There's no one else." She looked at her physician. "Nainai is old and not doing well. Please make sure she has a comfortable home until I can take care of her again."

Dr. Spellman assented, and turned to discuss things with a nurse who had just entered. Lacey turned her thoughts to Victor, who was pacing again. *What are you thinking?* she asked him.

His jaw clenched, he chose to speak with his mind too. *About what I'd do to your old boss if I were alive.*

She knew what that meant. *You'd beat him up?*

Well, maybe that too. He crossed his arms, perking up one brow.

What else do you mean, then?

I'd take Greg Mendoza, the man, down. I'd strip him of all his things. His job, his title, his illegal games and fortunes, his home, his wife—if he even really has one—get him arrested, and have him rot in jail.

Lacey coughed. She covered it with a fist, even though Victor couldn't feel nor contract a thing. *You're getting distracted. We're supposed to be finding your murderer, and take* them *down, remember?*

Victor shook his head at her with a smile that said, "You don't get it, do you?"

"*What?*" Lacey asked him out loud.

A nurse took Lacey's right arm, rubbing the inside of the elbow with alcohol. "Make a fist," she interrupted, eyeing Lacey dubiously.

Lacey complied, then returned her attention to Victor. She didn't even feel the sting of the antibiotic being administered. *What don't I get?*

"Oh, Lacey," Victor said vocally, kneeling at her bedside. "This is tearing me up inside."

Lacey frowned. *What is? Just tell me already.*

He leaned in, his face so close that she should still make out the little golden flecks in his eyes, despite his translucence. For a second, she wondered whether he was going to try kissing her. For another second, she wondered whether she would have welcomed it, had she not been feeling like death herself. But he didn't, and the moment passed.

Victor stood and resumed his pacing. "Here you are sick, or worse, and I can't do a thing about it." He paused, as if realizing something momentous.

Lacey almost thought she saw him trembling as he slowly turned large eyes on her. "What?"

"I just realized, if you ever end up in a scrape, there's really *nothing* I can do to save you. I can't even touch you." Just to prove a point, he strode to the bed and passed his hand back and forth through hers several times.

While Lacey still felt fluctuations of warmth it was, indeed, very obvious that he couldn't truly touch her.

"Don't ever do anything stupid, Lacey. Don't put yourself in danger. Promise me that."

Lacey rolled her eyes, and moaned at the small wave of pain that rippled up through her stomach. "You worry too much, Victor," she muttered, earning another curious look from the nurse. Then, in her head she added, *I'm a big girl. I can take care of myself just fine.*

It was Victor's turn to frown. "I already told you I'm not just hanging around Earth to nab the killer. I'm here to be with you. To protect you as best I can, even if that's not much." He growled. "I couldn't even protect you when Greg drugged you. Those… things were everywhere. I just can't handle Legion. The demons. But I can't leave you, either, Lacey. I can't let go…"

He sighed deeply, and buried his face in his hand for a beat, then he locked eyes with her again. The nurse and doctor finally left the room, but Lacey didn't watch them go. Instead, she watched Victor, remembering how close they once were.

"I never got the chance to propose," he said, "but my feelings for you will never die. I'm sticking around."

Lacey felt a flutter in her heart, but didn't let it show in her eyes. She knew she and Victor wouldn't have made a good pair, but to know that his devotions had survived death moved her deeply. She had to admit she'd be hard pressed to find another guy who she was sure would feel that way about her. "I promise I'll be careful, Victor. Let's just get me through this, and we'll take things one day at a time. Okay?"

Victor gazed evenly at her for a long moment, then finally nodded. "Okay. I love you, Lacey Ling. Heaven knows my heart."

She swallowed hard, knowing what he expected her to say, wishing she could honestly say it. She could see that he knew it too, but he was willing to meet her where she stood. Her eyes welled up with tears. She smiled through it, through all her pain, thinking for a moment that Nainai was right. Victor St. John was marriage material, after all.

Bursting the moment, he asked a chilling question. "What if Greg Mendoza is my killer?"

NINETEEN

The next two days passed with a strained slowness. Feeling trapped in her hospital room, Lacey argued with her doctor about an early discharge; the symptoms that had raked her guts the morning after Deborah's visit had cleared up very quickly. Dr. Spellman insisted that she needed to be contained, to prevent spreading the disease, and said that her bloodwork was still showing enough of the wrong signs. In the end, Lacey relented, and spent her days either talking to Victor (who found he could hole up in the hospital's chapel at nights) or mindlessly watching TV when he got too annoying.

The bright side was that she and Victor had plenty of time to discuss the possibilities of who may have offed him. Victor was reticent to leave Lacey at all, however, and though she insisted he go trail Greg during the day, Victor was equally insistent that he remain with Lacey and keep her company through the dragging hours of boredom not soothed by daytime drama.

Still there were problems with suspecting Greg. Evidence pointed to him having been in the US when Victor died; were that true, then the only way Greg could have been involved would be to place a hit for Victor.

"But why would he do that?" Victor asked for the

thousandth time, insinuating himself between Lacey and the drone of the television. "He didn't even know me."

Lacey rolled her eyes. "How should I know? I don't know how men think. You do. So... think. Consider again what made you suspect him in the first place, and let's attach a motivation to the murder."

"He gives off bad vibes, for one. For two, he is linked to both Japan and the Seattle area. And now I know he drugged you. Some dude broke into my apartment the night I was killed. It all went so fast. I-I couldn't recognize him. All I know is he was dressed in black. Maybe it was him or a hitman, maybe?"

Lacey nodded in agreement. "Okay. So the motivation could be?"

Victor shook his head. "Rivalry would be a possibility, but I was never really rivals with him."

"Except," Lacey interjected, "he might have a thing for me. Isn't *that* enough to get you males riled up and bashing one another's skulls in?"

Her dead ex huffed. "C'mon, Lacey. We're not *that* primitive. Though, I could see myself bashing his skull in if he tried something on you."

"Well," Lacey said carefully.

Victor flashed to her bedside, and peered at her with narrowed eyes. "I can already hear what you're thinking. And no, it's *not* a good idea."

Lacey pouted. "At least let me say it out loud."

Victor threw a hand up. "Fine."

Lacey's face screwed up in thought. "It's pretty obvious Greg *does* has a thing for me."

Victor muttered something like, "...break his fingers..."

"While I doubt he'd out himself as your killer, if he is, if I could get him to talk, I may be able to piece together enough clues to nail him—since you're so unwilling to just read his mind."

"I tried that once," Victor said, absently. "It was when we were in the helicopter with him, a few days back. I found I didn't want to stay; I've never been into the whole porn thing. And reading his mind may as well have been reading a Playboy magazine."

Lacey blanched. "That doesn't help, Victor."

He shrugged. "Full disclosure, babe. I'm more transparent than ever, these days."

She rolled her eyes. "At least dying hasn't murdered your sense of humor."

"Booo," he said. "Hey, look. I just said that. As a ghost."

"Can we cut the terrible jokes for a minute? I'm trying to think here, and trying to help you."

"Fine, fine."

Lacey pursed her lips in thought. "I'll meet up with Greg to see what information I can glean from him. I don't think it should be too hard if I take things to the next level, by pretending to be interested in him. But if he tries to use that perfume on me again…"

Victor nodded solemnly. "You're not sure you'll be pretending anymore."

Lacey shivered. "I promise I didn't kiss him, Victor."

He placed a hand gently on her shoulder. "I know. But even if you had, I would blame him for drugging you. I know you wouldn't do that in your right mind."

Lacey smiled up at him. "Thank you, Victor. For your faith in me."

He smiled back. After a pause, he leaned forward. Lacey's eyes grew wide as he continued to close in. "What are you doing, Victor?"

He smiled gently, and closed his eyes. "Just humor me."

Lacey made to speak again, but she felt the warmth of ghostly lips against hers. The sensation was both weird and wonderful, but despite her initial misgivings, she felt neither violated nor weirded out. It certainly wasn't like a real kiss, but the emotion behind it was as real as she'd ever known. And so she flowed with it, for a few seconds, letting his incorporeal lips caress hers, and remembering how it had felt back when they'd been dating. When he broke the kiss, Lacey found she'd actually been holding her breath.

Victor pulled back, smiling. His smile quickly faded, though, and Lacey felt her heart sink a little. "I'm sorry, Lacey. I shouldn't have done that."

No, you idiot, she screamed in her mind. *Don't ever tell a girl something like that.*

Victor's eyebrow's bunched. "Why not?"

Lacey stopped mid-word, then recovered. "It's *so* unfair you can read my mind. But since you can, then you should already know the answer to your own question."

He thought about it for a few moments, gently probing Lacey's mind—with her permission—until at last, the light bulb went on. "Ah. I see. Look, I don't regret the kiss. Not at all. I regret that I can't give you the real deal. I'm not going to lead you on."

Lacey pouted. "Then why'd you do it in the first place?"

An impish smile crossed his face. "You know you enjoyed it too."

Her frown deepened, then she smiled. "Yeah. Yeah, I did. But let's focus. I get out of here tomorrow, and I don't want to wait on this.

"I'm going to bite the bullet and use myself as bait for Greg. As soon as we figure things out, one way or the other, I'll drop him like a hot potato, even if I have to use the 'crazy chick that can't make up her mind' act. He'd buy that, I'm sure."

Victor again nodded thoughtfully. "I really don't like it, but I'm not going to talk you out of it, am I?"

Lacey rolled onto her side and took a sip of the juice on the food stand at her bedside. "Please don't try. I'm already doing it for you."

Victor acquiesced reluctantly, and the two finalized the details. Eighteen hours and a lot of paperwork later, Lacey Ling was a free woman again. With Victor at her side, she readied herself for battle.

TWENTY

"I think I have just the weapon to protect myself," Lacey said standing on her bare tiptoes. She was in her grand walk-in closet in the master suite of her luxury apartment, and pulled down one of the many shoeboxes stacked on the highest shelf.

"You're going to show me some new kicks?" Victor mused. "I know you like heels, but I doubt the effectiveness of even the sharpest stiletto at fending off a psycho."

Lacey shook her head, and simply lifted the lid, revealing a shiny pistol.

"You've been packing heat all this time I knew you, and I had no idea?" Victor stepped back with drama. "That's a bit surprising."

Lacey rolled her eyes. "Have I told you nothing of my family? My father?"

Victor replied, "Oh, I've heard plenty about Butch. The day you dumped me. Remember? 'You remind me so much of him.'"

"No," Lacey said, walking right through him, carrying the shoebox gingerly to her bed. "I didn't say you remind me of him. Dad is a redneck, taught me how to hunt; bought me my first gun when I was nine. In all those ways, you are not like him."

"Okay? Then what did you mean?"

"I was saying our relationship was like my mom and dad's. They're so different from each other. We're so different. It worked for them, but I envisioned something else for my someday marriage."

"Gotcha," Victor said, disappointed. "So you… are trained with that thing, huh?"

"Yes," she said. "I always felt safe enough on my own, so I never had it at my bedside. But," she said, grasping it by the handle, and looking at it solemnly from all angles, "things have changed."

"Well, if you're sure you can handle that—"

Lacey gave Victor a steely look of strength that shut him down. "I've got this." She lifted a leg, pulling up the hem of her red dress to reveal a thigh strap.

"That's… hot." His eyes lingered a little too long. He cleared his throat, snapping out of it. "Did your dad teach you that too?"

Lacey smacked at him, of course hitting nothing but air. "It's called a leg holster. And, no, the NRA did."

"I didn't know you vote Republican," he said. "There's something we have in common!"

"Geez, Victor!" She smiled. "Can we get serious, here, a moment?"

"I was!" He threw his hands up.

"Anyway, here's the plan, to recap…" She stood, pulling down her dress to her knees. "I'm meeting up with Greg at a neutral location, somewhere definitely safer than the warehouse. I'll still have my trusty sidearm on me just in case anything goes awry. The mission: to put my stuff to the test, see how well I can do with interrogating under a visage of innocence. I'll see if I can get him to divulge his feelings about you. I'll also test what his real interest in me is, which will let me know if I'm safe with him, so I can take my investigating to the next level. It will be just a couple hours, and so I'll be back in time to tuck my grandmother in bed without any hiccups."

Victor gave her a dubious look, but she ignored it and slid some black heels on, her hair cascading over her shoulders as she did so.

He sighed. "I just wish you were ready for a date with me tonight, rather than him."

"It's not a date," she said, and snatched up a clutch purse. "It's business."

*

Upon trailing Lacey and Greg into the restaurant, all Victor could think was *This definitely doesn't look business-y.* Their destination was dimly lit in pale pink and orange hues by sconced lights, artfully set between heavily draped windows. At only 8:00 p.m., it successfully gave a romantic ambiance of late evening. Tables were adorned by rich golden cloths. Chairs were upholstered in red velvet. Even the rug swirled with elegant patterns. It made sense now why Lacey was dressed to the nines. Every adult guest, as there were no children, was groomed like they were going to grown-ups' prom.

Of course the location was Greg's idea. Victor would have ground his teeth over the thought, if he could. At least the man didn't touch the small of Lacey's back as he led her to their reserved seating in a covert corner. Greg was good enough to slide Lacey's seat out, and she sat graciously, giving him a smile that was a little too real for Victor's taste.

Don't forget who died trying to propose to you, he thought at her. He felt her roll her eyes, but was impressed at how she kept it from showing outwardly.

The producer sat, and raised his hand for service. A waiter appeared a moment later, and Greg jumped at the chance to order wine, promising Lacey it would be the best she'd ever had. That made her think of Victor. Victor prided himself on picking the best wines ever. Lacey couldn't help but think how the fact that Victor was poisoned with cheap wine had added insult to injury. She imagined Greg dropping powder into his drink, that night. The thought made Lacey's face burn with anger. *If he did it, Victor,* Lacey sent her thoughts, *here's your chance to find out.*

I'm already looking into it, babe, Victor returned. Lacey smiled, and Greg, of course, thought it was all for him.

After ordering their entrees, Greg raised his glass. "How about a toast?"

"A toast to what?" she asked, lifting her glass.

"To you feeling better. To giving me another chance to talk with you about the future."

The way he said the future was flirtatious for sure. Lacey's toes curled with discomfort, but she decided she'd play a bit more interested tonight, to get inside his little brain. She knew Victor wouldn't. In fact, he had suddenly disappeared, surely not wanting to torture himself by watching every one of Greg's moves.

Greg sipped his drink, looking up at her with smoldering brown eyes.

Lacey politely smiled and took a drink. "What exactly do you mean by 'future'?" She humored him. "Do you strictly mean business?"

That question was obviously enticing to Greg. "There could be more… if that's something you'd be open to?"

Lacey played coy. "What about your wife? How are her headaches doing?"

Sucking in a deep breath, Greg's deep purple dress shirt strained against his muscular chest. "So there's some news there."

"Yes?" She couldn't read his expression.

Victor reappeared in an instant, frowning as he put a hand on Lacey's shoulder. *Uh, oh.*

Greg lightly pulled at his orange tie, and took another sip of his wine. "We actually signed divorce papers. It's been a few months."

Lacey put on her most intrigued expression and leaned in, eyes narrowed just right. "Really?"

"That got his heart rate up," Victor muttered. Lacey tried

to ignore it, but felt her skin began to crawl when her ex-boyfriend followed up with a growl. "Wow. This guy is *really* on the hunt."

Greg took another sip, and gazed back into Lacey's eyes. She saw what looked like real sadness, and it tugged at her heartstrings. "Yeah," he said. "She filed. I tried to talk her out of it, but the headaches really mess with her mind. She kept making things up, trying to make me look like the bad guy."

With a supreme act of will, Lacey managed to keep her skepticism in check. "That's too bad," she offered. "She must have said some *terrible* things."

"She *did*," Greg said perking up.

Lacey dropped her voice. "Probably even accused you of stuff you didn't do."

"Yes!"

"Sleeping around?"

Greg nodded vigorously.

"Illegal acts?"

"Several, actually."

Lacey leaned in conspiratorially, placing a hand on the table. Victor leaned in as well. "Even," Lacey whispered, "*murder*?"

Greg rocked back in laughter. When he calmed enough to talk, he reached out and placed a hand on Lacey's. She flicked her eyes toward it, then back at Greg, before giving a shy smile. Greg responded by squeezing her hand gently. "You're a ball, Lacey Ling," he said. "Hiring you was the best decision I ever made at KZTB."

Victor growled, wishing he could knock "Mister Television" into the following Tuesday. He opened his mouth to say something, but came up short. Something felt... off. Immediately he cast his eyes about for Legion but was relieved to see that, despite the dimness of the room and the shadiness of some of the patrons, the demons had not yet manifest for the night. Instead, there was something less sinister, but still clearly angry, and it was close. He began searching with his mind.

"I lost a good woman, Lacey," Greg said, half surprising her, and distracting Victor from his search. "I loved Deidre more than life itself. But the woman I married," and Lacey noticed the tears pooling in his eye, "she's gone now."

It was Lacey's turn to put a hand on Greg. She made soothing noises as she stroked the back of his palm.

"Easy, girl," Victor said, trying to remember it was all an act. He could still feel Lacey's sense of disgust roiling just beneath the surface, and it comforted him.

"Oh, Greg," Lacey said, "that is so sad. Maybe she didn't deserve you after all." Greg half smiled, but said nothing. "All those trips overseas—I bet she accused you of a lot of things when you got home."

He nodded without gusto. "Yeah. I tried to make it up to her every time, but it just didn't work. I spent a *ton* on gifts, Japanese clothing, chocolate, wine, and still she kept insisting I was sleeping with local call girls. Or even—get this—*staff*." He rolled his eyes and Lacey faked a laugh, trying hard to hide the fact her heart was racing.

"Let me guess," Lacey said, "she accused you of slipping something in their drinks and taking them back to your apartment."

Greg sighed heavily and buried his face in a hand. *Victor*, Lacey whispered fiercely. *Are you getting this? What's he thinking?*

Victor concentrated on Greg's thoughts; on the surface, they were flipping back and forth between how *good* Lacey looked and how it might not be a bad idea to slip something into *her* drink before the night was over. Again, he felt that strange sensation of nearby anger.

"Get away from this guy, Lacey. Before he does something."

Lacey pursed her lips, passing it off as sympathy. *Did you get proof, Victor? Did Greg poison your wine?*

Victor shook his head. "Not quite. But he's thinking about drugging *you*, that's for sure. Whatever you do, do *not* go home with this guy."

Lacey perked up immediately, and summoned a waiter,

who arrived a moment later. "Yes," she said to the woman, "can we actually get boxes for these? Something's come up, and we need to leave early."

Greg looked up in a flash, confusion plain on his face.

Lacey patted his hand. "I think we should find somewhere a little more private to discuss these kinds of things. I was just going to watch TV at home, after dinner, but something tells me you could still use a listening ear. My place? What do you say?"

Victor threw his hands up. "I just said *don't* go home with him. Not 'Take him to your house and pretty much invite him to do whatever.' What do you mean 'listening ear'? I don't even have to be a mind reader to know how he took that."

Lacey bit her lip and let her free hand caress the gun at her thigh just for comfort. Greg eyed her dubiously; she needed some better bait, and quick. "Look," she said quickly, "I'm sorry if that came off as a bit too forward. I just, well—I can tell that you really need a… friend… tonight. Food's still warm. Let's just eat it somewhere that lets us talk a little more… freely. Eh?" She sighed inside, and Victor groaned.

"Lacey, Lacey, Lacey. You're killing me. And *no* that wasn't meant to be a dead joke."

Greg bit his lip. "Well, the divorce *is* finalized, so no one can accuse us of anything." He chuckled nervously, and Lacey copied him. His face softened slightly. "Thanks, Lacey," he said sincerely, "I could really use a good heart-to-heart."

Victor's fists clenched instantly, hearing Greg's follow-up thought. As Lacey got up, Victor stepped right in front of her. "Do *not* take this guy home, Lacey. I'm telling you—"

Please, Victor, she said, stepping through him again, *trust me. I know a little about men. Just because you never figured that out while you were alive doesn't mean I'm a dunce.*

"Hey, Lacey?" Greg said, signing for payment. "Can we make one quick stop on the way back?"

Lacey hesitated, then smiled. "Sure. How about we take my car? We'll pick yours up in the morning."

Greg smiled wide. "Now that's one of the best ideas I've

heard all night."

TWENTY-ONE

Lacey's heart hammered as they pulled into the parking garage at the KZTB tower. Night had fallen early under a thick bank of Seattle's best cloud cover. Greg had been silent most of the trip, but, thankfully, had also kept his hands to himself. Aside from the occasional glance at her, and a few directions, he may as well not have been in the car. Victor, of course, spent the whole trip rattling off the sordid details of Greg's thoughts, none of which included anything about Victor, cheap wine, or murder.

Hoping to tease out details, Lacey had brought Victor up a couple of times, but Greg offered terse, almost bored answers with barely the right amount of sympathy in them. His ambiguity was nearly infuriating, but Lacey maintained her coy, flirtatious act just enough to ensure Greg's interest didn't wane. She was starting to wonder whether this whole thing was for nought. Still, something inside drove her on.

As if to reassure her of his "friendship," he hopped out of her car the instant she parked, and hurried to get her door. Victor was there first, of course, with a look that Lacey knew meant, "I would have been here first anyway." Lacey smiled gently inside, and placed a hand on Victor's arm, even knowing she wouldn't feel it. His face softened, and he moved to let her pass.

"So, Greg," Lacey said, scanning the parking lot. Most of the day staff had gone home, but the place was far from empty. Yet the glare of fluorescent lights on the zombie-like parked cars did nothing to ease her nerves. "We go out to dinner, and your idea of a romantic epilogue is more office time?" She chuckled, but Greg only gave a weak smile.

"I guess I could have picked a better place, but I've got my reasons. Let's get up to the helipad."

Lacey arched a brow. Victor snorted a warning.

Greg half smiled. "You'll see."

*

The helicopter waited on the roof like a predator, silent and patient as Lacey and Greg approached.

"I know how you hate the wind of the rotors," Greg said as he helped her into the passenger's seat, "so I figured I wouldn't call ahead to have it started when we arrived."

Lacey gave him an appreciative look, and put a hand to her chest. "That was so thoughtful of you, Victor."

Greg frowned. "Come again?"

Lacey paused, feeling the blood drain slightly from her face. "I meant Greg. Sorry. I guess talking about my ex got him lodged in my mind. Like a chicken bone, or something."

Greg half chuckled. "Well, don't take it personally if I accidentally call you Deidre, or something, tonight." They both laughed at that, but Victor wanted to howl and to tear the guy limb from limb for what he was thinking.

"Oh, and thanks for indulging me that little stop in the office," the producer said, as he climbed into the cockpit.

"What little stop?"

He smiled. "I'm teasing. I just checked in with someone when you stopped to use the ladies' room on our way up. Standard procedure before checking out little pieces of equipment like company helicopters."

Lacey humored him with a laugh.

Greg set his headphones in place and Lacey did the same. The man started flipping switches all across the control panel.

Lacey didn't like how he suddenly had the upperhand, that he was taking her somewhere out of her control. Was she making a huge mistake? Even if she found no evidence to believe he was Victor's murderer—which was looking increasingly likely—she was sure he was still a criminal. And as a criminal, she doubted his scruples. The thought of the TV exec flying her to a remote location to rape her came to mind. Victor concurred and she shuddered.

Victor was now surprisingly resigned to not talking, taking a spot behind her.

"Well," Greg said, "let's get going. We've got some things to talk about." He turned and locked eyes with Lacey. "And I need your opinion on something important."

Somehow she doubted that…

TWENTY-TWO

Victor groaned as the chopper neared Greg's warehouse again. Chilling memories of his last visit to this place haunted him, and he wondered if he remembered the way to that Catholic church he'd taken shelter in—the one in which he'd seen Mr. Taniguchi dressing down the mousy accountant.

Meanwhile, Lacey was truly absorbed in what her former employer was saying. Almost as soon as they were in the air, the floodgates had opened about his concerns over his partnership with Mr. Watanabe. He explained that he'd taken the helicopter just to ensure that no one would be listening in or watching them, and mentioned that he'd let a trusted individual in the office know where to look for him in case he disappeared.

"That 'little stop'?" Lacey asked.

The man nodded. "Yeah."

"He's lying," Victor said abruptly. "But he's not thinking about whomever he actually saw, so I can't see what the truth is."

Lacey made a note of Victor's comment.

"Anyway," Greg continued, "Orochi is an *astounding* businessman; I've got to give him credit for that. But in case you missed the implications of what I've said," though Lacey knew very well what Greg had implied, "I'm just going to spell it out: I think he's in with the Japanese mafia."

Lacey gasped as expected. "Greg, why would you think something like *that*?"

Greg frowned as he steered the helicopter over the warehouse's roof pad, but didn't put the craft down. "A lot of things. Emails, faked checks, hints of drug deals, various comments. Even a few deaths."

Both Lacey and Victor perked up at that. "Deaths?" Lacey asked, eyes wide.

Greg continued to let the helicopter hover. "Let's just say that I'm not sure all his books are legit. He and his buddy, Taniguchi, well, there's something you should know about stockholders: they expect to see a return on their investments. But in real life, things fluctuate. You have good quarters, you have bad quarters. These days, though, stockholders don't want to *see* bad quarters. It's self-preservation to, you know, make some tailored alterations to one's financial records."

"You mean, cook the books a bit," Lacey said.

Greg cocked his head and shrugged. Lacey didn't like how flippantly Greg dismissed corporate fraud, but she kept it to herself and nodded like she agreed.

Victor leaned between the seats. "Ask him how many times *he's* cheated the system, Lacey."

Quiet, she hissed at him.

"Anyway," Greg continued, "Orochi's becoming a liability. And a threat. I need to make a quick, clean break with him before he drags me into criminal territory against my will. Territory that would put my own life at risk."

"Listen to this guy," Victor scoffed. "As if he wasn't already in deeper than a submarine."

Lacey frowned. *Will you* shut up, *Victor?*

"C'mon," Greg said, finally letting the chopper descend. "I've got something to look into in the warehouse. And I'm going to want your eyes on it."

*

The warehouse was, thankfully, demon free. Victor noted that it was not long past 9:00, but he'd seen Legion out as early as mid-dusk in certain parts of town, and then there was that one at the jewelers he hadn't been able to explain. On his guard, he followed Lacey and Greg through the bowels of the dimly-lit structure, absently wondering why there was no security presence until he noticed that Greg had had the good sense to have some surveillance cameras in place. Turning his mind back to the woman of his dreams, he immediately picked out her spike of nervousness as they passed a crate labeled "perfumes."

Greg paused and looked at the crate, then turned a smile on Lacey.

Lacey kept her cool, hoping Greg couldn't hear her heart slamming against her ribs. "There will be time for fragrances later," she said playfully, before putting on a stoney face. "For now, business."

Greg grinned. "Always so focused. You really will do great with my morning show. And with this business," he said, gesturing around. "I should have picked you up a long time ago."

"If you so much as touch her…" Victor growled.

Lacey broke the tension by taking a few steps forward, into an intersection of aisles. "So, Greg, what is it you wanted me to see?

Greg stepped up to her and stared for an uncomfortable length of time before answering. "It's there in the back. With the parakeets."

Lacey blinked in worry.

The KZTB manager's brows bunched. "Something wrong, Lacey?"

She nodded openly. "I have a… bad history with parakeets. It seems I'm allergic to them." She pushed back against the memory of clinging to her toilet bowl for a half an hour, wishing she could die.

"Ah," Greg said knowingly. "Well, I have just the thing.

Stay here."

Lacey complied, and not a minute later, Greg returned with a pair of hospital-style facemasks and some foam earplugs from a bulging pocket. He handed a set of protective gear to Lacey and slipped his own on. "I have to admit, the birds have been in pretty bad shape since they got here. That screeching makes me want to claw my eyes out. And I don't know what's up with their eyes, but all that dust, it makes me gag too. And don't you tell anyone about that," he added, jabbing a finger at her in mock accusation.

"Of course not," Lacey said. "At least not right away. I have to have *some* dirty little secret to leverage against you." She winked, then laughed. Greg laughed with her, but Lacey could see the tightness around his eyes, and immediately knew that he was accustomed to being betrayed; and she suspected he'd done a little betraying himself. That in mind, she quickly slipped on her mask, and gestured for Greg to lead the way.

Two minutes later, they stood before the dull collection of crates, the shrieks and smells of the parakeets kept at bay by Greg's countermeasures. Lacey stepped up to the nearest crate, and placed a hand next to the image of the child stapled onto the crate. Victor came up next to her, and he felt himself pause. "That kid looks familiar, Lacey."

Lacey opened her mouth to speak, but caught herself. *What do you mean "familiar"?*

"Like, I've seen that face somewhere before. The name, too; it rings a bell."

Well? Lacey said, hiding her impatience from Greg under a guise of thoughtfully peering at the image.

"Well," Victor replied, turning to peruse the other boxes, "I think it's a good thing I'm here with you to have a look around."

Greg glanced at Lacey, just then. "What'd you find?"

Lacey frowned. "I don't know. It's hard to tell much by just a picture, a name, and some Japanese characters. My kanji was never very good."

Greg arched an eyebrow. "So, is that your feminine way of

saying, 'Greg, get a crowbar'?"

Lacey gave him a small smile. "Not exactly, but, since you do own this place, it wouldn't be illegal. And let me guess, you already have a crowbar."

Sure enough he held one up. A sudden tremor went through Lacey's mind. They were alone. A single swift blow from that thing might be all he needed to put her out. What would he do with her then? Chuckling nervously, she took a casual step back, trying to pass it off as her wanting a wider look at the crates. After a moment, she locked eyes with him. "Well?"

Greg gave her a wicked smile. "Eager to see how well I can use my equipment, eh? All you had to do was ask."

Lacey's throat went dry. The implications of his statement disgusted her, but she knew she couldn't give it away. She *needed* the information she was sure he could give her. She forced herself to be calm inside. *You can do this, girl*, she told herself. *You're strong. You're smart. You're amazing.*

With another smile, Greg went to work on a crate. "See, this is actually a big part of why I brought you here. Hang tight, and I'll explain in a sec." Nails groaned as he worked the crowbar into a groove, then began to lever it back and forth. "See, Orochi always told me he'd been shipping stuff to orphanages, and to charities that helped victims of human trafficking after they'd been rescued. He's pretty smart about it, too. Uses multiple different Japanese banks to house his funds, which means he can donate anonymously. You wouldn't think it, but he's actually a pretty charitable guy. Or, at least, he *looks that way*. He's been storing these crates here for months. Something tells me there might be something inside them that isn't as good as he's made me think. I'd like to find out before he screws me over by surprise." He went quiet and resumed his work on the crate.

Lacey felt a faint ripple on her skin that came with Victor's ghostly touch. "You are, you know," he said. "Strong, smart, and amazing. I wish so much I could have married you."

Lacey turned away to hide a blush. She hated blushing,

especially where others could see. *Now's not the time, Victor. And anyway, aren't you supposed to be in church, or something?*

Her dead paramour frowned. "Normally I would be. This place was *swarming* with demons last time I was here. If I go silent without warning, you'll know I had to run. Those things don't give much notice that they're coming for you. But when they do, you can't miss their intent."

Lacey bit her lip. *I'm glad you're here now, at least. Have you figured out why that kid looked familiar?*

A crack of splitting wood and a shrill groan of nails announced that Greg had nearly opened the box. Victor and Lacey both stole a glance at his progress, then Victor spoke up. "I'm glad you asked. I have figured it out, and now I'm *insanely* curious to know what's really inside these boxes. Curious and nervous, that is."

Lacey raised her eyebrows. *Oh?*

Victor pursed his lips. "The last few weeks of my internship I kept finding these random stashes of money. Each one was supposed to go to help some random orphan kid. The money all had notes, and they always said the same thing: 'Take this money to such and such a bank and deposit it for this child.' Totally fits with what your old boss just said."

The look on his face told Lacey that he'd swallow the lump in his throat if he could, and he was silent for a moment. *Well?* she pressed.

"Well," and he looked over as Greg triumphantly jerked the lid off, releasing a shower of sawdust. "I get the feeling I may not have been contributing to charity after all."

Greg swore, and Lacey's eyes went wide. The guts of the crate were filled with small plastic bags of white powder, desiccated; brown plant material and cash. Whole wads of cash.

Victor groaned. "You've *got* to be kidding me. I was laundering *drug* payments?"

Lacey's breath caught. "Greg, are those—"

Her former boss nodded fiercely. "Orochi was setting me up." He turned to Lacey. "I brought you here as a material witness in case I need to testify. You saw me open the crates, and you can tell how surprised I am by all of this. He waved an arm at the findings. "He violated our deal, and he violated my trust. I'd had a suspicion that he was looking for a way to exit me from the business so he could take my share. Looking at all this, I think I know what he had in mind. All Orochi would need to do was—" He stopped suddenly, his ears perking expectantly. Lacey and Victor copied him, but Victor shook his head after only a moment.

"I don't hear anything," he said. "Not sure what he's listening for, but I'm only getting the usual sounds."

Lacey eyed Greg, pretending she hadn't heard Victor. "Am I missing something?"

Greg frowned, then sighed. "Knowing Orochi, he would have had the cops already on their way. I guess I was expecting them to surround the place and find us in the middle of all this," and he gestured at the crate. "He'd lose a big chunk of cash in the short run, losing this merchandise. But with me in jail, and him taking my cut, it'd be chump change in the long run. I bet he's got more inventory in his other warehouses to make up for losing this one. He'd do that, too. That sly son of a gun. Well," he said, a chilling grin forming on his face, "turnabout is fair play, right?"

Lacey's heart raced again. She wasn't sure what he had in mind, but she didn't think she wanted to find out. In her gut, she knew he was probably complicit too. But how to prove that? Nerves squeezed her bladder uncomfortably.

Greg pulled out his cell phone, and Victor concentrated on his thoughts. After only a second, Victor locked onto the man's plan. "He's calling the cops, Lacey. Going to turn in Mister Watanabe on an anonymous tip. Ah. And—wait. Taniguchi? That's right—he said he knew they were partners. Wow. I'm glad I'm around to see this."

While Greg dialed, Lacey touched his arm gently. He looked up at her, then smiled stiffly. "Hey," she said, "where would I find the ladies' room?"

Greg raised his eyebrows. "You went just before we came

here. How much did you have to drink at dinner?" She blushed, and he chuckled, then pointed. "Down that way. Just keep going until you find the office. Pass that, and then the second door on your left."

"Thanks. Back soon." Hurrying away without a backward glance, she heard Greg start to speak. If he was trying to set a trap for his partner, Lacey didn't want to be in the middle of it. She'd have to hit the bathroom quickly and make it back in time to get out before the cops arrived. Yet, as she jogged past the office, she noticed the door ajar. Curiosity got the better of her, and she peaked in.

The place looked like any other dockside office she'd seen, and she eased through the door and snatched at some of the papers on the desk. After scanning them for a moment, her eyes widened. In just a few pages, she found information that would easily implicate Greg in money laundering, human trafficking, and even, possibly, murder. "My, my, Mister Mendoza," she muttered. "We've been a bit sloppy about hiding evidence, haven't we?" Why such papers would be lying openly on his desk boggled her mind, but maybe Greg had been right—maybe Watanabe really had set things up. If so, planting this kind of evidence in the open would be sure to land a swift conviction for the head of KZTB.

"Lacey?" Greg's voice sounded from beyond the door. Starting, she rammed the pages into her purse, and dashed to the door. Peering carefully out, she found she was clear, and bolted for the women's room, easing the door shut behind her. She took care of business quickly—as much for an alibi as for comfort—then made a show of washing her hands, certain he'd hear the running water. She emerged nearly a minute later, playing on the male idea that women always took forever in the bathroom.

Greg, of course, was waiting just outside, a mixture of satisfaction and worry on his face. "Wow," he said. "You got out of there quick. Good thing, too. The cops are on their way. Best that we take off." His face softened. "Besides, the night is still young."

Lacey giggled nervously, not sure how far she wanted to go with this. She was nearly certain, by now, that Greg had had nothing to do with Victor's death. And yet, she'd just found some real dirt on him—something she couldn't, in good conscience, walk away from. She was already in too deep for comfort. She needed to get away from him, and that meant playing along for just a while longer.

Greg stepped closer and took her hand. She felt a sticky sweat on his palms, but checked her disgust and let him continue. "We outsmarted him, Lacey. And I couldn't have done it without you. He lied to me about what was in those crates, and I should have trusted my gut and checked sooner. But we've got him now. I'll let the cops deal with this." He turned to leave, and tugged at Lacey's hand.

She resisted. "Wait a second, Greg."

He turned back to her, impatience clear in his eyes. "We need to leave. I don't want to be here when the police arrive."

"But, Greg—"

He shook his head sharply. "No buts, Lacey." He wrapped both her hands in his and held them up. "Trust me here, Lace. I've totally got this." He removed his respirator mask and brushed his lips across her knuckles. Lacey couldn't hide the way her face flushed. Greg, of course, seemed to take it as bashfulness, instead of fury, but Victor was clawing at the guy and screaming about what he'd do to him if he were alive.

"Let's go, Lacey. I don't want the evening to end this way. And," he said, a fox's grin curling his lips, "I'm pretty sure *you* don't want that either. Besides, we haven't even finished dinner."

She swallowed hard, but steeled her mind and nodded.

"Babe," Victor said, "you *know* where this is going. Ditch this guy *now*. And—wait a second—did he really do *that*? Lacey he—oh, no. No, no, *no*. Not them *again*."

Lacey actually felt Victor's presence depart, and she couldn't help but whirl frantically to try finding him. She caught a glimpse of him flying up and through the back wall, and then there was nothing. At least, until a cold, dark presence seemed to spread through the area. She shuddered, and Greg clasped her hands tighter, a new warmth spreading from her palms and slowly up her arms. Oddly, she found she half enjoyed it.

"C'mon, Lace," he said sounding a bit tipsy. "Chopper One isn't going to fly itself back."

The thought of doing this alone, without Victor, kicked her anxiety up several notches.

TWENTY-THREE

The ride back left Lacey feeling increasingly heady. She wondered why she'd been so nervous in the warehouse. Something about Greg's nearness beckoned. Seattle's nightlife slipped by below her, couples under streetlamps, patrons filing into bars, cars wandering wherever they would. She wished she were down there with Greg, instead of still up in the air. Indeed, Greg was almost drunkenly amorous on the return flight, stroking her hands and face frequently, leaving trails of fire in the wake of his touch. She found she was enjoying it more and more, but the visceral pleasure mingled with naked disgust and a growing sensation that bordered on panic.

Despite Greg's appearance of confidence, she was sure the police would implicate Greg when they found a warehouse he owned filled with illicit substances. She couldn't help but think that he'd drag her down, too, if things went south. Even more troubling was the fact that she couldn't believe that he *was* actually innocent. She knew she was walking a razor's edge, and held no illusions that things might not turn ugly in an instant.

So why was Greg's constant touch so enjoyable?

It wasn't until they landed, and Greg cut the engine to let it idle itself to sleep that Lacey realized just how *good* the man smelled. He climbed out, and hurried over to help her. As he ran around the front of the helicopter, she noticed him stuff his hands in his pockets again, and wondered at the way he rather gingerly opened the door. Still hoping to stay in character, she took his hand—still moist with perspiration—as he helped her down.

Yes, he *did* smell wonderful; and it was rubbing off on her.

Rubbing off... Her eyes widened as realization dawned, and she was so distracted that she gave no resistance when Greg's arm snaked around her waist and he led her away from the helicopter. Not toward the stairwell, but toward the opposite corner of the roof. His hand filled the small of her back as he guided her toward the parapet surrounding the roof. He stepped in next to her, pressing his flank against hers as he looked down on the street.

"It's pretty," he said simply. He turned to look at her, and she felt his eyes on her. "But not half so pretty as my little Asian delicacy."

Lacey giggled half-heartedly. She wasn't sure how much longer she could keep up this act. Worse, she was already feeling the effects of whatever was in Greg's cologne; he must have had some in his pocket earlier. Whatever it was, it was *undeniably* powerful. The night seemed to glow as her eyes dilated, and she felt warm all over. She *craved* the sensation of his fingers on her face and hands. But her conscious mind knew it was all a lie, and she struggled to break free as her mind harked back to the time he'd used spiked perfume on her. Then, in another breath, her worries began to fade again.

"I'm sorry about the warehouse," he said sincerely. "I didn't want to do that, in the middle of our date, but it just seemed right. I knew I could trust you, and it had been burning a hole in my mind for two weeks. Now that that's over, though, I'm still game for the offer to go back to your place. But can we just have a moment, here in the dark, just you, me, and the city?"

Lacey bit her lip. "It's getting late, Greg."

He chuckled. "It's not even ten. The night's just getting

172

started."

She shook her head. "I'm not sure I can do this. Not right now. I mean, what we saw back there. It shook me. I'm going to need some time to process this."

In turn, he slipped his hand in his pocket again, then pressed his palm to her neck and held it there, pulling her toward him. Her pulse soared, and her head fought with her hormones. She jerked away abruptly, and took a definitive stride away from him. "I can't, Greg. I wanted to, but things have changed. Just give me some time." She turned on a heel and walked quickly toward the stairwell. "I do business better when I'm not worried about incarceration."

Greg was in front of her in a flash, bodily blocking her retreat.

"Greg? What are you doing?"

His hands settled on her hips. "Lacey, all night long you've been telling me how you really feel about me."

"Greg," she said, trying to pull away, "I'd *love* to do business with you. I'm just—"

"Business," he said huskily. "I know exactly what kind of 'business' you're interested in." He stroked her cheek, fiery lust in his eyes. "Imagine what we'll accomplish together."

His face moved in closer to hers, his musky cologne calling to her on the night air. Her face was frozen in surprise, her lips parted. He pressed his mouth to hers. It was warm and soft, and her body screamed for it, though her heart pounded her chest in protest. Her mind struggled against the drugs, but whatever Greg was using, it was too strong. Taking fistfuls of Lacey's long black hair, he kissed her deeper, pressing his body against her.

Lacey pulled back to get air. She reached into her purse and clamped her fingers around the files from Greg's office, slightly shaking. She *needed* these files, this evidence. But she also needed Greg to stop feeling so supercharged. "Let's just… cool our jets a little." She smiled weakly.

"What are you waiting for? I'm an eligible bachelor. I own all… this." He spread his arms, then gently squeezed Lacey's arms. "You know how many women want me? How many of your co-workers want me? Deidre was actually right about that part; the women wanted me, and with Deidre's condition, well… a man needs his outlets. Deidre was none the wiser, and I improved staff morale. Ask Janae how much she enjoyed it. Lisa. Even Deborah; she succeeded… quite a few times." He raised his eyebrows a touch in pride. He was clearly intoxicated.

"Wh-why would you tell me that?" She was repulsed.

He fingered a lock of her hair. "I'm just letting you know what a hot commodity I am. I want you to want me, and actually, I know you do. It's just, this playing-hard-to-get act you've been doing is driving me insane. I have urges, needs. And tonight, you look"—he gave a husky groan of approval—"like a *goddess*."

Shaking herself free of the intoxication, she stepped back in her heels, her right ankle wobbling. He stepped forward in pursuit, but she continued her retreat until her upper thigh hit something. Quickly glancing over her shoulder, she realized she was against the roof's ledge again. Wind rustled her hair, unsettlingly. And although a horn honked only ten stories below, it sounded miles away.

She couldn't very well grab for her gun, and she wasn't about to anger Greg at a moment like this. He was a pawn she might still need, to at least close the illegal operations if she couldn't use him to solve Victor's murder.

"Greg," she said, softening her expression as best she could, "I'm just feeling a little lightheaded, being so high up."

Suspicion crossed his dark eyes, before he chuckled. "You're a pro at flying along in my helicopter." He put a hand behind her waist, pulling her forward, away from the ledge but against him. "Better?"

Her thoughts jumbled together, and the world began to spin. She staggered, but Greg caught her, then buried his face in her neck. His lips flamed on her skin, but instead of being pleasant, it caused her guts to roil. Without warning, she shot her wine down the back of Greg's collar.

He jerked back in shock.

"Oh! Oh, no, Greg. I'm soooo sorry," she said. A little giggle bubbled up, robbing her apology of any sense of sincerity. She couldn't help it, and giggled even harder as the effects of whatever he'd used on her mingled with the alcohol from dinner. Apparently, Greg wasn't the only one dealing with the inebriation.

He cursed loudly, and stepped back, just in time to catch a second barrage of vomit to his polished loafers. "Ugh! Oh! My—*ack*!"

"Greg, forgive me. I—" She continued to laugh. "I'm sorry, really." She reached a hand forward to wipe off his lapel, smearing and making things all the worse.

"Forget it!" He backed away, disgusted.

Lacey slumped to her knees. "I swear to you there was nothing I could do," she drawled, then giggled some more, because in her state of mind it was just too funny.

"Do you have *any* idea," Greg demanded, retreating, "how much this suit cost me?" Any trace of lust was gone from his eyes, but she felt no fear at the anger that had replaced it. "I'm going to need to change. You just stay right here. We'll finish this later."

Lacey feigned compliance for the sake of getting rid of him, and he stalked off, muttering and swearing under his breath. As he ducked into the stairwell, it occurred to Lacey that she'd accidentally stumbled on the time-honored defense of skunks; that made her laugh even more. "That's how I *really* feel about you, Greg Mendoza. You swine."

Feeling immensely better, Lacey reached up and grasped the parapet, using it to haul herself to her feet. The taste of bile stung her mouth and lingered in her nose, but she was so grateful to have avoided something far worse that she couldn't bring herself to mind. She glanced down at her red dress; surprisingly, only the smallest drops of colorful spittle had dripped on her. With trembling hands, she pulled a handkerchief out of her purse. After a quick clean up, she filled her lungs with the salty-sweet night air, and headed for the stairwell.

"Stay right here my foot," she said, wondering what had happened to Victor. She wished he'd been there for her ordeal; surely his howls and threats against Greg's life would have kept her from giving in so much to what must have been contact drugs.

Moving quickly, but still unsteadily, she slipped into the stairwell and, with a firm grip on the railing, started her descent. She'd take the elevator as soon as she could, to hopefully reach her car before Greg learned she was missing.

Her thoughts were interrupted by a tone from her cellular. She pulled her phone out and noticed a cryptic text message. "You're barking up the wrong tree," it said.

Lacey narrowed her eyes at the message and thought of Victor's ex-girlfriend, Jessica. The woman had told Lacey that same thing at the airport. The context had been different, back then, but the parallels were unmistakable.

If this was Jessica, stalking her with a vague message, what did she mean? She hadn't spoken to the woman since the airport. It didn't make any sense. Victor had assured her Jessica knew nothing about his death.

Ding. Another message: "It wasn't your boyfriend who was supposed to die."

Lacey's heart pounded, adrenaline coursing through her body. She quickly scanned her surroundings. The stairwell was dimly lit. There were lots of shadows. She pulled up her dress, sliding out her gun. It was cold in her hands.

Ding: "It was you."

TWENTY-FOUR

Holding her gun low as she stepped quietly along, she called out in her mind, *Victor! Where are you?! Victor! Come back! Please!*

He appeared next to her, concern showing across his wrinkled brow. "What is it? I got here just in time to see Greg—"

"I just got some texts saying that the murderer was after me."

"After you? As in right now, you mean?"

"The wine was meant for me," she spat in worried frustration. "They wanted to kill *me*." She lifted her gun a little higher, rounding a corner. Her chest shuddered in short breaths. "I need to calm down," she told herself. "I need out of here. I need to tell the police everything."

Eager to reach the nearest elevator, she holstered her gun and hustled back upstairs. She pushed open the door leading to the 10th floor, only to slam it shut almost immediately. "He's coming *back already*?"

Victor stuck his head through the door—which Lacey found disconcerting—then reappeared and met her gaze. "And fast. Maybe another few seconds. Looks like dinner didn't agree with him. He's got puke all over himself."

177

Lacey instantly weighed her options. Exiting into the floor's hall to catch an elevator was no longer an option, and she was certain he'd see her if she went down another floor. The door to the roof was only half a flight up, but that would leave her trapped. When she heard footsteps just outside the door, instinct drove her back up the stairs toward the roof before she could think.

Ding. "I know where you are."

Lacey froze, her hand on the push bar of the roof exit. Should she respond?

Ding. "I'm coming for you. You're mine, slut!"

Was this just some sick joke? Was it safer to be inside, with Greg hot on her heels, or outside where she had nowhere to go? The slam of a door, one flight down, made up her mind.

"Lacey?" It was Greg. "I told you to stay put." A split second later, heavy feet pounded up the stairs behind her.

She shoved the door open and ran onto the roof, the night breeze suddenly chill, her only company being the sleeping helicopter. Searching frantically for a place to hide, she realized her only options were to take either cover in Chopper One, or hide behind the stairwell structure; neither option would conceal her for more than few seconds. That left her with only one *good* option. Whirling, she grabbed for her gun just as Greg hurled open the door.

The gun stuck in her thigh strap.

Greg flicked a glance toward the weapon, his eyes widening in comprehension. His nostrils flared, and he charged Lacey, blasting her onto her back before she could make a second attempt to unholster her gun.

"I take you for a night on the town," he said, dropping on top of her and slapping her again and again, "offer you your own show; think about making you a partner in the biggest business venture I've ever done, and *this* is how you repay me? You really think I'm that stupid, Lacey? You were just using me. Just like my wife; like Orochi; like all those other women." His hand snaked up her skirt, and she rammed her heel into him, earning a groan of pain, and another slap. He repositioned himself to avoid her kicks.

"Well, I'm still getting *something* out of this deal," he spat, his meaning obvious. One hand gripped her neck while the other roamed her, hungry. The reek of vomit, mixed with cologne, assaulted Lacey's senses. His knees dug painfully into her shoulders and she was starting to see stars. Her self-defense training was lost in a jumble of panicked thoughts.

Victor stood helplessly by, wishing he could wrench Greg off and hurl him from the roof; he checked the thoughts quickly, though; Rao hadn't been kidding when she'd told him how negative emotions called to Legion. Already he could see a black haze forming around the roof. He'd been supremely lucky to evade them once, tonight; he wasn't certain if he could do it a second time. And yet, he couldn't leave Lacey. Nor could he bring himself to watch.

"Lacey," he called, kneeling beside her, fighting tears, and doing his best to interpose himself between her and her attacker, "just hold on, baby. Keep fighting him. Don't give up! Kick, scream. Do whatever!"

Lacey was already ahead of him, but her efforts were clearly in vain as Greg continued to strangle her toward unconsciousness. Lacey knew what would happen once she blacked out, and renewed her struggle. For a moment, she even managed to lever him off her with a surprise roll to her side. Yet she rolled onto her gun, and by the time she was able to twist the other way to reach it, Greg was on her again.

As Lacey watched the world dim around her, she prayed— the way Victor used to. In fact, she felt him praying *with* her. She had no idea whether it would work, but she could *taste* "desperate" in a way she'd never even imagined.

A sharp crack rang out in the air.

Greg jerked, stiffened, and then slumped forward, flopping bodily onto her. His grip slackened instantly, and Lacey sucked in a deep, welcome breath despite the stench. Rolling Greg off her, she saw a dark figure in the stairwell doorway. Her blurry vision kept her from making out any details, but it seemed that whoever it was, was pointing at her.

Another crack, and her ears started to ring slightly. Whoever it was, was shooting at *her*. Instinctively, she rolled, and out of sheer desperation ripped her gun from its holster. Barely bothering to aim, she squeezed off three rounds, stunned at just how *loud* a gun was when she wasn't wearing hearing protection; no wonder Dad had always insisted on it.

Though she was sure she hadn't come anywhere close to hitting her new assailant, she saw a wavy image of a person hastily retreating into the stairwell. Taking only a moment to catch her breath, she staggered to her feet, and let adrenaline take over. Sprinting awkwardly for the stairs, she stepped to the side of the door, careful to stay behind it and yanked it open. When no gunfire erupted, she hazarded a peek inside.

It's safe, Lacey, Victor said in her mind. At least she could still hear that. Lacey rushed inside, and peered down the stairs. The dark figure was half-leaping down flights, and Lacey knew she'd be hard pressed to catch up. Down and down they went, the murderer clearly bent on outpacing Lacey, and certainly preventing a good shot. "Who *is* this person?" she said, half breathless as she watched another floor flash by.

I'll go down there and find out who it is, Lacey. Don't chase this guy. He flashed away in an instant.

Ignoring Victor, Lacey continued hurtling down the stairs, gun still in hand.

Victor caught up with the perpetrator just a few floors up from the basement. Whoever it was, they were dressed like a ninja, swathed in tight black fabric from head to toe. Victor's eyes widened when he noticed the figure was definitely feminine. He reached into the woman's mind, only to be rebuffed by a cacophony of emotions and a million disparate thoughts. He tried a second time with the same results. A darkness seemed to surround her, and Victor felt the uncomfortably familiar sensation that seemed to herald Legion's arrival.

"I'm not leaving Lacey *this* time," he growled. There *had* to be a way to fight them. Ceasing his failed efforts to read the woman's mind, he flashed back up to Lacey who, surprisingly, had nearly caught up with her attacker.

Lacey paused, angling her gun to get a sure shot. She pulled the trigger, and a bullet ricocheted off something metal, the sound zinging loudly in her ears.

"Careful!" Victor called out.

The person in black haphazardly fired back, hardly even glancing over their shoulder as they continued their descent. Lacey ducked just before a bullet hit the wall beside her.

Breathing hard, she stuck to cover. Though it kept her safe, it let the murderer escape from view. Glancing at the hole in the wall beside her, she caught her breath at the near miss. "You're not going to get away with this!" Lacey said, before peeking over the railing. Two flights down was a bodily shadow on the wall. If she were right, she'd get another, clear shot any second now.

Pointing her gun over the edge, she did what her dad always taught her: her elbows locked, breathing steadied Although her heart pounded, she aimed quite precisely at where the enemy's back would appear. This would be Lacey's last chance at having the upper hand of the stairwell; they'd nearly reached the basement.

She watched and waited. The moment came with the black blur dashing away. Her finger mashed the trigger. The recoil shot through her arms and out her shoulders, and her target jerked, as if they'd tripped on something.

Lacey's eyes widened, eager to see whether her stumbling attacker had been hit. Instead, the murderer recovered their balance, and dove for a nearby exit into the basement. Before Lacey could get another shot, the dark figure awkwardly flung open the door and disappeared into the darkness beyond. Did she get them? Pulling off her high heels, and tossing them aside, she stepped cautiously down the stairs.

Victor shivered as a small clutch of demons swirled out of the walls and hastened after the killer as if inexorably drawn to her; he counted his blessings that they hadn't seemed to have noticed him. He grimaced as he felt his resolve to stay with Lacey begin to slip. "You don't have to go after her," he said with a pleading voice.

"Her?"

Victor nodded. "Yes, it's a woman."

"You sure?" The figure had been on the smaller side, but events were unfolding too fast to make out much else.

"Um, yes. I am fairly positive by my up-close scrutiny of her black blouse," he said dryly.

Lacey frowned. "I really didn't need to hear about you examining other women's blouses, Victor."

He shook his head in frustration. "Not like that. Just that tight fabric tends to show a woman's figure."

Lacey bit her lip, and hurried forward toward the door. "Jessica?"

"I don't know." His face flashed in thought. "A $22,000 engagement ring doesn't really make sense, in that regard. And we ruled her out a while ago."

Lacey shrugged. "Maybe she bought the ring for herself and was waiting for you to propose?"

"Even for Jessica, that seems like a huge leap in irrational thinking. Why would she kill your boss? Or try to off you?" He stepped in front of Lacey with his hands up, stopping her. "Listen, you don't have to get into a gunfight. I can go follow her, find out who she is, where she goes. I don't want you to get hurt."

"Victor, once again you are questioning my capabilities. I am ready to do this. We may not get another chance. In fact, I can be set up as Greg's murderer. Some of my old coworkers saw me here with him. I would be the target. Now if you don't mind, I'm going." She stepped right through him and directly toward a door posted with a sign reading, "Keep out. Authorized personnel only."

Lacey gently opened it and peered inside at what was simply darkness. Victor first peeked through the door, knowing Legion could be lurking behind it. He could see everything he needed to tell her where they were at: A mechanical room. A very large mechanical room.

He drifted inside with dread. Where was Legion?

Watch your step, he mentally cautioned Lacey as she entered quietly, gun still drawn. "There are tons of electrical cords in here," he added aloud. "Your boss should hire better maintenance staff; OSHA would have a fit if they saw this."

Lacey frowned. "Do you have anything more useful to add, Victor?"

He shrugged. "I'm going to look for the she-devil. This place is full of hidey-holes." He caught her eye, and put on his most pleading look. "Just please be careful. I *love* you. I want to be with you, but not at the cost of your life."

Lacey didn't respond. Instead, she slinked by a shelving unit hosting various gadgets with red or green lights, some blinking ominously at her. This was probably the only space in the entirety of the KZTB tower she hadn't ever perused, besides the men's bathrooms. Her feet padded over a couple cords snaked across the cold concrete floor; she sucked in a breath in surprise, and kept moving.

A deep hiss and a gust of air made Lacey stiffen, and nearly jump. From somewhere in darkness, she saw a sliver of blue flame burst to life near the floor, but she couldn't make out details. The initial rush of sound subsided, leaving an eerie semi-silence buzzing in her brain. Lacey rounded the corner of the first row of shelving to the next, and mentally asked Victor, *Well? Where is she?*

"I'm looking," he responded. It was strange. Though he couldn't see Legion, the residue of their passage lingered, stifling his senses, and stirring panic inside him. He fought to keep it down, knowing that fear would draw the creatures to him like sharks to blood. He literally flew over several shelves, circled the entire perimeter of the room—a few times—and still didn't see anyone. "She's not here."

Are you saying she just up and disappeared?

"I... guess I am." He hovered nearly flat against the ceiling, eyeing it all. "But how? I don't see another way out."

But Lacey, although not a spirit like her ex, also sensed evil close by. A chill at the nape of her neck told her so. *She's here, Victor. You're not looking hard enough.*

"I don't—"

He was cut off by the faint sound of… what was that? A doorknob?

TWENTY-FIVE

Lacey whirled toward the noise, and saw, through the dimness, a door farther into the room, bearing a sign reading "Boiler Room. Authorized Personnel Only." Below it was the sliver of blue firelight she'd caught a glimpse of earlier.

"Now how did I miss *that*?" Victor asked. His senses were even duller than he'd realized. Legion's presence was nearly palpable now.

Checking to ensure she was clear, Lacey bolted for the second door, pausing just outside. Sounds of metal on metal echoed from within the room beyond, and Lacey frowned, wondering what was going on. "Victor?" she asked.

"Already way ahead of you," he said, even as he flashed through the door to reconnoiter the next room. He practically leapt back into Lacey's space a heartbeat later, and though he wasn't actually gasping, Lacey could tell he would be, if he weren't dead.

"There are so many of them," he said, his face drawn. "Whoever that chick is, she's a *magnet* of dark things. Stay out here. Just call the cops and let them deal with this. See? If you take cover behind that machine over there," and he pointed at a large piece of equipment, "you'll still be able to see the door, and if she comes out, you fire off a couple warning shots to keep her honest until help arrives."

Lacey held in a pout. "Why do you *always* doubt me, Victor? Even when we were dating, it was, 'Here, Lacey. Let me help you with that.' Or, 'I've got this, Lacey. You just sit tight.' I'm so *sick* of you telling me I can't do things. As wonderful as you can be, I couldn't stomach the idea of living life as a 'cute little China doll' who just sat around on display like a helpless baby."

Victor gaped. "W-wait. You mean, you were *offended* by my attempts to be a gentleman? I was trying to *help* you because I *loved* you."

She shook her head. "Are we *really* having this conversation right now?"

Victor glanced back at the other room. Though the banging sounds continued, the murderer was making no obvious moves to come out. He turned back to Lacey. "Yeah. I think we have a minute."

Lacey rolled her eyes and threw up her hands. "What do you want from me, Victor? Do you *want* some 'good little wife' that will clean up after you and cook you meals and look pretty when your friends come by? Why do you insist on treating me like I'm weak and stupid?"

Victor was flabbergasted. "I let you have all sorts of personal freedom. Ask yourself if I was like any of your past boyfriends—like that one dude… Buck? Chuck?"

Lacey leveled an unimpressed stare at him. "Roland."

"Whatever. Remember how he had to know *everything* you were doing every minute of the day?"

Lacey shifted her weight, and glared at her dead ex-boyfriend. "Why do you think I dumped him inside a week?"

Victor waved it away. "Look, I gave up *Heaven* because—"

He was cut off by a particularly large bang from the other room. Before he knew it, Lacey dashed across the room and hurled open the door. A curtain of steam blasted outward, and she reeled back with a yelp, only to throw herself forward again. She trusted her gut; she could *sense* Greg's killer inside, and knew that the steam would give her just the right element of surprise.

"Lacey, *no!*" And yet, the overwhelming sense of fear emanating from Legion paralyzed him.

Victor watched in horror as she dove through the door, heedless his warning. He watched Legion swarm her instantly, and felt the crashing waves of doubt, fear, and confusion they tried to drive into her mind like railroad spikes.

Lacey, for her part, pressed doggedly forward, ignoring the unexpected deluge of doubt. Something told her to turn left, and she did. Two steps later, she tripped over something on the floor and stumbled forward. To her surprise, she collided with something soft—something that let out a feminine scream.

"Gotcha!" Lacey cried.

The woman—at least Victor had said the murderer was such—struggled against Lacey. Lacey whipped her gun forward to take a shot, but the other woman fought dirty, stunning Lacey with a blow to the head that she didn't see coming, before grabbing at her gun arm. The two struggled in the steamy darkness, Lacey fighting to keep the murderer's gun out of play while her opponent did the same. There was kicking, screaming, hair pulling, rolling on the floor. By sheer force of will, Lacey heaved her gun toward the other woman and pulled the trigger. The woman must have seen the move coming, because she dropped bodily onto Lacey just as the gun fired. The bullet ricocheted off an overhead pipe—which added another jet of steam to the mix, then hit something somewhere else.

The lights went out.

A punch came out of nowhere, and Lacey felt her head rebound off the concrete floor as stars exploded across her vision. Swinging blindly, her counter-attacks met with nothing but empty air. At once, the despair she'd been swimming in since entering the room crescendoed to an overwhelming pitch.

You've failed, Lacey. She's better than you, and now, she's going to kill you. You'll get to see your beloved Victor soon, though. But when you do, you'll find he hates you for dishonoring his sacrifice. He gave up Heaven, and now that you're about to die, you've consigned him to Hell.

Give up, Lacey. It's too late to change.

"No," she wanted to shout, but it came out as a weak cry. Over the hiss of steam and the intermittent pop of damaged electrical equipment, she heard the familiar click of a round being chambered in a pistol. All the stories about one's life flashing before them at the moment of death proved true. Lacey closed her eyes and sucked in a breath, hoping her death would be quick and painless.

Yes, her thoughts said. *There is no purpose in going on. Go to Victor. Go to him.*

"But I don't *want* to die!" The thought infused her with adrenaline and she rolled instinctively, only to immediately ram her head into something metallic and immovable in the darkness. Six gunshots rang out. Through the murky haze, Lacey saw a demonic figure, clothed in black, highlighted by the flash of each shot. And then there was only darkness.

*

Still stunned by his girlfriend's thoughtless bravado, and frozen by terror, Victor could only stare. He heard half a dozen gunshots ring out in rapid succession. Any hopes that Lacey had survived died when the killer emerged—limping, but still clearly alive—from the boiler room, trailed only by fewer of the demons than he'd seen follow her in.

The woman in black jerked the door closed, then put another bullet through the locking mechanism; Victor had a sinking suspicion the knob would no longer work. Struggling to get control of his emotions, he gritted his teeth and willed himself forward. The terror was still there, though, and he barely made headway toward the boiler room. If Lacey were dead, her spirit would still be inside, trapped with whatever Legion members were left. He couldn't leave her to that fate.

"Rao? *Rao?* Where *are you*, you stupid cat?"

No reply.

"I *need* you. *Lacey* needs you! Please!"

Still silence.

The murderous woman left the mechanical room, trailed by a dark entourage, and the pressure eased at once. Victor flashed through the boiler room wall, eager to find his love. No sooner had he materialized in the boiler room than a lingering demon pounced on him, raking its icy claws through his thigh. He screamed and fell back, anger welling inside him.

Yes, the dark ones hissed. *Anger. Yesssss!*

Two more turned for him, but in the half second he had before they were on him, he spotted Lacey, lying on the floor, pressed up against a large water heater, her spirit nowhere to be seen. Then they were on him. It was everything he could do to duck, dodge, and weave around their attacks. For whole minutes the dangerous game of cat and mouse went on, over and around the unconscious form of the woman he loved. One beast caught hold of him and flew straight up through the ceiling, Victor fighting to break free, and held him until they the KZTB tower looked like a model train building below them. Several others were right behind. The demons struck with ferocity, but he realized they were not coordinating their attack when two of them got into a scrap as one tried to pull the other out of the way so as to reach Victor first.

He frantically tried remembering Rao's instructions, desperately tried to resurrect pleasant emotions and the type of courage and faith she'd said he'd need to combat them, but it was useless. Unable to find his girlfriend's soul, he knew he'd lost already. He'd have gladly accepted his fate had he been able to go down defending her, but Legion had denied him even that hope. Desperate for one, last touch, he dove through the remaining demons—earning wicked, stinging wounds in the process—shot back down into the basement, and collided with Lacey.

Only, he was stunned to find himself repulsed. He bounced back, racing to her to see how bad the damage was. His heart sank when he saw blood on her head, and on the ground. Then, he noticed that the dark liquid trailed toward the door. "I'll be," he mused for a split second. "Lacey actually got her." His thoughts died under a renewed demonic assault.

Without warning, Lacey jerked once, then twice, then groaned and slowly attempted to sit up. Legion halted as one, their attention fully occupied by the woman on the boiler room floor, and for the first time, Victor noticed the shell casings scattered around, and the pockmarks of bullets on the floor near where she lay.

Victor's heart lifted instantly. "You're *alive!*"

Lacey wasn't sure whether she'd lost consciousness or had merely been stunned by the resounding blast of the gunfire in the close quarters. Blinking repeatedly, she felt as though she could hardly breathe. Her ears threatened permanent tinnitus, but she could still hear Victor's triumphant call in her mind.

"Yes," she said weakly, coughing on steam, "I think so, at least." She coughed again, then froze. On the humid air she could practically taste the sulfurous odor of natural gas. "Victor? Victor, I've got to get out of here."

Legion exulted, and Victor grabbed for Lacey instinctively, only to be frustrated to find that he couldn't help her. One demon detached from the rest and came for him, but Victor was ready, this time, and managed to catch the monster's flailing arms as it lunged for him. The rest of the creatures seemed fixated on the lovely, living lady before them. Victor could feel Lacey's mind weakening.

"Victor," she said blearily, already feeling herself beginning to swoon, "how long have I been… down here? I think… the gas is… getting to me." She struggled to get to her feet, but collapsed to her knees; the blows she had taken fighting the other woman seemed more severe, now that she was off her adrenal high. Her head throbbed mightily, and when she gingerly touched the place where her head had hit metal, her fingers came away smeared red. Rising again, only to stumble anew, she pushed on into the darkness, only to meet a wall face first.

Victor opened his mouth to guide her, but as he did so, the demon he was struggling with turned to vapor, and shot into his mouth. He gagged for the first time since dying, and struggled to spit it out. He could see the entire boiler room as though it were midday; Lacey, however, was heading in the exact opposite direction from the door.

Lacey, he thought. *You're going—*

Legion! the demons roared, cutting him off. The beast that was worming its way into him began clouding his mind, misdirecting his thoughts; he'd never seen them do this before, and Rao hadn't talked about it.

Feeling her head growing lighter, Lacey stuck to hands and knees as she searched for a way out, feeling her way along a wall, reasoning that eventually, she'd find the door by following it. The steam burned at her face, and several times, she touched metal that seared her hands, causing her to cry out and lose her way.

It's over, Lacey. Lay down. Rest. You've done your best. The police will catch the killer, and if you're not around to be implicated, so much the better. Victor is waiting.

"Victor," she called, before coughing again. "Victor?" Her knee hit something, and she was sent sprawling the floor, her face slapping concrete.

Yet, Victor's struggles were just as insurmountable as hers. Thoughts of Lacey asphyxiating filled his mind. He envisioned her succumbing, collapsing, and her beautiful spirit rising out of her dead husk, only to be assailed by the powers of darkness. He pictured himself becoming one of the demons, and then going on to ravage her pure soul like all the others. He would drag her down to an endless misery the likes of which he was only beginning to comprehend.

Summoning all his will, he made to rage against Legion. Then he stopped. *No*, he thought. *That's not what Rao taught me. That's not what* Mom *taught me.* He remembered all those old religious songs he'd listened to in life. About courage, faith, resolve to do right in the face of evil. Though it wasn't much, he began to sing, a new sense of calm filling his mind. The demon that infested him shuddered violently, and redoubled its mental assault, but Victor latched on to the song, and

191

began putting his heart into it. Forcing his mind to be calm, he felt the parasite beginning to ooze reluctantly out of him. For once, he could actually think clearly. But Legion wasn't done yet. The invader fought back furiously, and it was all Victor could do to keep himself on track with singing, and thoughts of saving Lacey. Pushing back even harder, he forced the demon clean out of his space, and created enough mental space to allow himself to talk.

"Lacey," he called, both aloud and to her mind. "You're almost there, baby. Just crawl forward two feet."

The monsters roared in unison. *NO!*

Lacey, ears still ringing, and vision blurred, felt her heart rise at Victor's encouragement. She complied as best she could. After what seemed like an eternity—all the while filled with a whirlwind of doubt and logic about why she should quit—Victor's words came again.

"Great job. Turn ninety degrees to your right—to your right—and keep going. You're only about ten feet from the door. That's it, baby. You're doing great."

No! No! Go to Victor!

And then they were on him en masse, ripping, tearing, gnashing with fangs he didn't even know they had. His internal singing faltered, and his focus on Lacey blurred dangerously. The darkness enveloped him as it had the night he had died, and he felt himself being dragged away from Lacey.

"Lacey! No! Get off me!" Thrashing and struggling in vain, he watched the boiler room vanish above him. He was being pulled down, down, growing colder by the second, and weaker. All sense of time vanished. His forced descent may have lasted a minute, but it may have lasted a thousand years. He thought of Lacey, gasping and struggling above.

You've failed her. Failed!

And they were right. He had failed. A desperate cry ripped from his throat. "Rao! Rao! I need you! I—" His thought was suppressed under a crushing burst of mental white noise. The cat failed to appear; he wasn't even sure she'd heard him. His thoughts faltered further, and soon, he could hardly even envisage Lacey's beautiful face in his mind. The thought of losing her split his heart in two. He'd given up Heaven to be with her, and now—

Then it hit him. Heaven. So he committed to the last, best sacrifice he could make for her.

God, he managed to cry in his mind, *I'm sorry. Just let me help Lacey this once. I'll come home then.*

Legion shrieked, a screeching that sent pain reverberating through his very being. Then, quietly, but with increasing speed, the pain began to subside. Now it was the demons that were thrashing and flailing. Their grip slipped away, and he felt as though he were sucking in a breath after coming up from a deep dive. Indeed, he found he was beginning to *glow* the same way Rao did. A smile crossed his face, and he turned to regard the cluster of dark ones who had already retreated a pace. Instinctively, he pointed at them and in a calm, but firm voice, said, "Be gone."

With a last, ear-splitting shriek, the entire mass of Legion fled into the bowels of the earth. Victor exulted in his deliverance, his smile widening as he watched his enemies run. He only spared a moment on his triumph, then he was back in the boiler room the next.

Lacey was barely dragging herself forward by now. "Victor?" Her voice was weak, and she barely got the word out before coughing again. "So... tired... Vict... where?"

"I'm here, baby. You're almost there. Scootch just two inches to your left. That's it. Now just go straight. You can do it. We're safe now." Yet he knew that *she* was anything but. Kneeling at her side, he continued his encouragements as she inched forward, the strain clear on her face. She'd talked about gas; Victor knew she'd been down here too long already. A new realization dawned on him. "Vents," he said. "There should be some."

It took him all of a half second to fly the perimeter of the room. There were, indeed, two vents, each with fans. To his dismay, they both showed clear evidence of what he was sure was recent damage. Suddenly, all the banging he and Lacey had heard made sense. He bit his lip. "She was set up."

Blinking back to her, he urged her on. "C'mon, Lace. I know you're tired, but I'd love it if you could give me just a little more speed."

She nodded weakly, and he could sense her strength of will in each inch she covered. After nearly a minute, Lacey bumped up against the door. Groping upward, she eventually fumbled across the knob. She turned it, but it felt strangely hollow—the way her head felt now—and nothing happened.

Victor put his face *into* the door mechanism. Sure enough, the killer's bullet had disabled it. "I'm going for help, Lacey," he said, slipping through the door and back into the main mechanical room.

Lacey felt her heart sink. "Don't... don't... leave me... Victor." She blinked against a growing headache, her lungs already burning fiercely. The smell of the gas was overpowering, but she couldn't think clearly enough to guess how much longer she had. All she knew was that it wasn't long, and that she wanted Victor—a clown, a buffoon, and a knight in shining armor all at once—to be with her now.

Hang tight, he called to her mind, sensing her slipping. *Stay alive, Lacey Ling. For me.*

"Vic—" Her word broke into another coughing fit.

Wasting no more time, Victor sped through the building, desperately searching for someone to help Lacey. He encountered several security guards, but none seemed to be even the slightest bit able to hear him. He tried the after-hours editorial room, but the KZTB staffers were so caught up in preparing the morning news program that his pleas were completely unnoticed. Fortune finally favored him when he happened upon a grizzled old maintenance man, frowning at a control panel in one of the lower levels. A flashing red light seemed to occupy him, and his concerns were clear. Victor locked on to the man's thoughts as best he could, and went for it.

"There's a gas leak in the basement," he said. "A woman is

trapped in there. Call the cops, the fire department, whoever, or do it yourself. Just do it *fast*."

The maintenance guy perked up, and looked around as if someone had spoken to him. Victor felt his spirit rise. "Gas leak. Basement boiler room. Go!"

"I'd better get downstairs, pronto," the man mumbled. He sniffed briefly at the air, and his eyes widened. He turned and raced down the hall, pulling the nearest fire alarm on his way. Strobes burst to life up and down the hallway, accompanied by the anxious wail of the fire alarm.

Victor had to admire the maintenance man's bravery. He followed his mad dash down four flights of stairs, and into the mechanical room. He was glad the man had the good sense not to flip the light switch, but to, instead, pull his beefy Maglite from his belt before donning a respirator.

Victor was grateful to sense no sign of Legion in the vicinity; he had beaten them completely. Then he caught a faint ripple of Lacey's thoughts; she was still alive, but fading. "Hurry up, dude," he urged.

The technician cautiously felt the door with the back of his hand, then, satisfied there was no fire, tried the knob with no success. He paused for thought, then raced across the room to a tool rack, where he grabbed a heavy, rubber mallet. Though Victor was dubious, the technician was dogged and surprisingly strong. The man hammered at the metal knob until Victor heard something give. At once, the old man dragged the door open, and an unconscious Lacey Ling slumped at his feet. Relief washed over Victor, until strange whispers of light started emanating from his ex's limp state.

"Oh, no," he said taken aback, grabbing at where his heart once beat. "Oh, no. Please, God—no. No, no, no…"

The maintenance man cursed under his breath, wiping his brow, and immediately scooped her off the ground. He ran for the door, shouting for help. Victor's sense of conquest died in an instant, replaced by the most bitter guilt. He hurried after the maintenance man, stopping only when Lacey was set down in a safe place, whereupon the man jerked off his respirator and immediately began CPR.

By now, the whispers of light had intensified into a full bodily glow, and then Victor watched as a true angel crawled awkwardly up and out of the shell of his former girlfriend.

TWENTY-SIX

Stunned and confused, Lacey wondered why she suddenly felt fine. The room, once impossible to see in, was now nearly as bright a noon day. The doubt, fear, and naked panic that had seized her mind were gone. She felt more alive than she could ever remember. Glancing around the room, she found she'd somehow managed to escape the basement. Something caught her eye, and she glanced down to see an old man hunched over a lifeless woman. Almost instantly, she recognized that woman was *her*. "No," she said quietly. "No, I can't be dead." She staggered backward and immediately bumped into something warm. She spun with a gasp, and was rendered speechless by the sight of Victor—as visible as he'd been in life—standing there.

Victor's heart broke at the sight of Lacey's big brown eyes, wider than ever, shining up at him. They fixed on his, begging for answers. "I-I'm so sorry, babe," he mustered, as he surprisingly felt something trickle down from his eye.

Lacey's gaze trailed the shimmering teardrop cascading down his cheek, followed by another. Her bottom lip involuntarily pouted out. "Oh, Victor," she threw her arms around his body. It felt like a real hug. No, better than that. It was the most warmth she had ever felt, like being wrapped in the softest fleece blanket, from head to foot. She snuggled in closer, and Victor obligingly tightened his embrace, clinging to her like a drowning man.

After a long moment, Lacey broke the embrace and gently pulled slightly away. She reached up to stroke Victor's face. "It's not your fault. Don't blame yourself."

"How can I not blame myself? I got you involved with this mess from the start." He lovingly took hold of her forearm, his dark brows pressing together in anguish.

Lacey shook her head. "Remember, the killer was actually after me from the start. She just… finally succeeded."

She smiled at him with pure charity. Victor couldn't suppress a modest smile of love in return. "Your sweet cinnamon sprinkles are glowing," he mused softly.

She laughed, her lips broadening. His gaze flicked toward them, and she found she knew his thoughts perfectly.

"Hey," he said, "you already let me kiss you in the hospital. I'll be even better this time." Her smile grew coy, and she found she liked the idea. Tilting her head up, she let him lean in. His lips met hers, as they had in life, and though it seemed trite to say it, the kiss was literally heavenly.

When they finally separated, she actually giggled. He, of course, wore his usual, impish grin. "Wanna try that again?"

She swatted him playfully. "Hush, Victor St. John." They shared a laugh, and a look. Death wasn't nearly as frightening as Lacey had expected. "What now?" she asked, speaking of their next phase.

"I don't know… Do you have any former pets?"

She paused. "A beta fish named Bennie."

"That ought to be interesting." He peered up at the ceiling, as if awaiting its arrival.

As if on cue, and to both their surprise, Rao showed up, descending on a little white cloud, her striped, furry arms crossed. *Alright, alright. I'm here. You two should get a room.*

"Ms. *Tibbits*?" Lacey burst.

Victor turned a wry smile on Lacey. "I told you I wasn't crazy."

The name's Rao, honey, the feline said with attitude. Lacey was surprised to hear the voice in her mind; the cat never once moved her lips.

"Oh, excuse me," Lacey said. She then said out of the side of her mouth at Victor, "Sounds kind of sci-fi, like a robo-cat to me."

The cat cut in. *Hey, hey, hey. Don't diss the name. It's cool. At any rate, I'm here to help Vicky Boy make good on his promise.*

Victor sighed, resigned, then perked up. "Wait—she can come with us, right?"

With you? *Victor, Victor, Victor. I take people to paradise. And you want her to spend an eternity with* you? *Break out the fire and brimstone, why don'tcha?*

Lacey laughed. At once, the reality of her departure set in. Her expression fell as a new dread crept into her heart. "Wait What will happen to Nainai?" Her eyes then bounced between Rao and Victor. The cat quirked an eyebrow, but Victor was clearly at a loss for words. Disappointment and guilt warred in his eyes.

"I-I'm not ready for death. I'm not ready. I-I can't leave now. I have my life. I have my grandmother."

Rao said, now eye-level with her, the cloud dissipating, *That's the struggle every righteous being has when crossing over. Those they leave behind; those they love…*

Victor's strong gaze pulled Lacey's eyes to his, and it all became clear.

Lacey's heart melted at the revelation of his devotion. "I understand now. I understand. Thank you, Victor."

He simply nodded.

"But, still, really," Lacey contended, "I can't leave my Nainai."

The fluffy black and gold angel said, *Lucky for you, you don't have to… this time.*

And in the next breath, Lacey's spirit was pulled back into her body by an unseen force. Immediately, she felt a sharp pain in her ribs, something pressing hard into her. Her eyes fluttered open before a bearded mouth met her lips.

She sputtered in surprise, and the maintenance man recoiled in shock. "You're alive!"

Lacey sat up with a gasp. The warmth and peace she had felt with death were replaced with the stench of gas, and pains all over her body. Before she could process the abrupt and unpleasant change, strong arms scooped her up, and she felt herself being quickly hauled from the mechanical room to the tune of a fire alarm.

Victor made to follow, but was restrained by a surprisingly strong, if gentle, tug on his elbow. He whirled to see Rao still floating there, eyes expectant. "But," he said, "she still needs me."

Rao's eyebrows lifted. *What was that you said a few minutes back? Oh, yes. And I quote, "Just let me help Lacey this once. I'll come home then." Sound familiar?*

Victor pursed his lips. "I'm still on that 'just this once' part."

Rao gave him a supremely incredulous look. *You're a real winner, Vic. You know in your heart what you meant. And we both know you're too honest to go back on a promise. Especially one like that.*

His shoulders sagged. "You're right." He sighed, the sense of loss slowly seeping through his body. And yet, Lacey was alive. Literally miraculously. He'd been granted his wish, and he wasn't going to whine about the price he'd chosen.

"So do I get to say one, last goodbye to her?"

Rao smiled knowingly. *You just made out with her. I think that counts, even if you didn't know it was your last goodbye.*

Victor opened his mouth, then thought twice.

Smart man. Rao turned as if to leave. From above, a shaft of light appeared penetrating the ceiling as if it were open to the sky. Faint, lovely music drifted down, comforting Victor, encouraging him to leave the world he knew behind and take the next step into another.

Rao gestured at the glowing conduit. *And now, you've got a little journey waiting.*

Victor looked up into the light. Were he alive, he knew it would be more blinding than staring at the sun. Instead, it was merely pleasant, happy, welcoming. "Just like that, huh?"

She nodded. *Just like that. Although you were too dumb to come willingly the first time.*

"And Lacey? Her attempted murderer is still at large. That makes it a bit harder to leave."

The cat's smiled widened. *Oh, we've got that covered, don't you worry. And give Lacey some credit too. We'll… give her some ideas, but trust her to be smart enough to pull 'em off.*

Victor stared at his former pet, then nodded, somehow knowing she was right. "I'm going to hold you to that. I want to see Lacey in Heaven—soon—but not if she gets here from unnatural causes."

The tabby moved away, and called over her shoulder. *No one dies of unnatural causes, Victor. They just don't know what the plan is. Just trust me.*

Victor pursed his lips, and watched as Rao sped away, disappearing through a wall. He waited a long moment, thoughts still locked on the woman he loved. She'd been here, dead as he was, just minutes ago. It had been all he could do to restrain himself from trying to talk her out of going back. And yet, he'd loved her enough to let her go.

With that, the music seemed to grow a little more pronounced, and a little more inviting. "I love you, Lacey. I always will. Don't get yourself killed, but know that I'll be waiting in Heaven when you arrive."

With that, he stepped into the light, and, drifting upwards, finally released her.

TWENTY-SEVEN

Clutching her head, the effects of the gas fumes refused to let Lacey go. After stridently insisting that she was fine, and required no more attention, Lacey had simply walked (or, rather, stumbled) away from the old man who had saved her life. Though she wasn't gaining strength fast, and though she still hurt all over, she managed to keep her feet, sucking in deep lungfuls of fresh air as she made her way out of the KZTB tower.

Immediately she was assaulted by flashing red and blue lights, and the noisy press of nervous people huddling outside in concerned confusion. A few police officers were trying to direct the crowd further away from the building as several firefighters suited up in SCBA gear. A police cordon was being placed, and she spotted a few officers standing nearer the building, clustered around a motionless form, and taking notes.

In a flash of insight, she knew who the body had belonged to. "Greg." She bit her lip, but suppressed her natural curiosity to see what had become of the man who had thought to rape her less than an hour ago. Her top priority was finding the woman who had nearly killed her twice.

Lacey searched the crowd in vain, but knew before she

started that no one was going to be seen in public dressed like a ninja. Lacey's only real lead was that her assailant was female. Dismayed, she pressed herself into the throng, hoping against hope that she'd find even a small clue—maybe just more of the blood she'd seen trailing on the floor leading back to the boiler room. That trail had ended quickly, and at any rate, Lacey hadn't been able to follow it for all she was being carried away from danger by a helpful older man. After several minutes of questioning the bewildered bystanders, she got nothing more than a vague comment about some woman having a limp as she exited, though Lacey's informant hadn't seen the woman's face, and was too busy thinking about getting to safety to pay any more attention. Frustrated, and finding no one limping in the crowd, Lacey turned back for the building, ducking under the freshly-placed police tape.

"I'm sorry, ma'am," an officer told her, catching her by the elbow. "Restricted area. Seattle FD confirms we have a gas leak. If you'd please move farther from the building…"

She reluctantly complied, and faded back through the crowd, trying to contemplate how she was going to get back into the crime scene. An idea flashed in her mind, and she skirted around the crowd of after-hours employees until she found one of the cameramen she knew only by sight. She knew he'd be the perfect accessory for the plan forming in her mind almost as if by magic, and maybe even for a contingency, if it came to that. She hurried to him, and tapped his shoulder. He turned, and regarded her at first with surprise, then with veiled admiration.

Lacey didn't waste time rolling her eyes. "You're on the nightly camera crew, right?" He nodded, clearly confused. "Can you access your camera without going into the building?"

He raised an eyebrow. "It's in the van…" he said, vaguely gesturing.

"Great. I need to borrow you. You can take me out for a drink, later, as payment. Here's what we're going to do…"

*

Straightening her hair, and double checking to ensure her mic was clipped on and hot, Lacey was ready. She nodded at the cameraman, and a red light on his equipment kicked on. "Good evening. I'm KZTB's Lacey Ling, reporting to you live from our own tower here in downtown Seattle where a *stunning* development has occurred." She gestured to the side, and the nameless cameraman dutifully panned around, taking in the police tape, the shimmer of emergency vehicle lights, and the slowly dispersing onlookers.

"As you can see," she continued, "the building has been evacuated. Official word is that a gas leak has occurred inside the building. Employees have been asked to return to their homes and as you can see, they're doing just that."

She signaled the cameraman to bracket her again. When the lens was on her, she put on her most somber face. "Though no injuries have been reported, it appears that a suicide has occurred, with a man apparently having thrown himself from the tower." At that, the camera pivoted toward where Greg's corpse lay, and zoomed in. Lacey held her breath, hoping her gambit would work.

"Though there has been no word from officials as to the likely motive of the suicide, police are investigating the possibility of a connection between the death and the gas leak. Terrorist activity has not been ruled out, though officials do appear to have contained the leak," and she knew she was making that up whole cloth, "meaning that Seattle's finest have averted what may have been a terrible, terrible attack."

She straightened, fighting not to wince as she did, and put on an air of satisfaction and triumph. "We'll have more to come, and I'll be right here, on-site, with coverage throughout the night. For KZTB News, this is Lacey Ling."

The red light disappeared, and the cameraman set his equipment down gently. Lacey thanked him, got his name, and made arrangements to check back for another broadcast in a half an hour. In the meantime, she could only wait, and hope the right person had seen the broadcast. She'd put the bait out; now she needed to stay put and be easy to find.

A movement caught her eye. Turning, she saw Deborah stumbling in her direction. She whirled to greet her, and was shocked to see the woman's red, puffy eyes and lack of makeup; she looked like an entirely different person. Just beyond arm's length, the perky show hostess tripped, but caught herself, then flung her arms around Lacey and squeezed, bursting into tears.

"Oh my *word*, Lacey! You're here. You're *here*. I can't believe this has happened!"

Lacey gently eased the weeping woman away, eyeing her. "Well, it was just a gas leak and an apparent suicide. I know they'd just raised our health insurance premiums, but jumping off a building seems extreme, don't you—"

"Don't joke at a time like this, Lacey," Deborah cut in. Glancing at the cameraman, she took Lacey by the elbow. "Excuse us, please."

Lacey complied, and allowed Deborah to lead her to a dark, quiet corner of the parking lot, away from the lights and noise. She sucked in a breath, and, clearly verging on another breakdown, jabbed a finger toward where Greg's body was being covered by a white cloth.

Deborah pursed her lips and squeezed her eyes shut. After a few moments, she managed to whisper, "That suicide was… that was *Greg*." Then she lost it a second time.

Lacey gasped. "Our *boss*?"

"*Yes*," the brunette hissed through clenched teeth. Lacey's arms came up to comfort the woman, but Deborah surprised her by wincing, and shrugging her off fiercely. "Don't *touch* me!"

Lacey recoiled, stunned. "Oh, I'm sorry. I was just—"

"No," Deborah interrupted, "don't be sorry. It's my fault. I just—Greg… he…"

Lacey felt her heart soften toward the woman. "He was your friend, wasn't he?"

Something flashed in the other woman's eyes, and another

sob bubbled up. "Can we," she stammered, "can we go back to my apartment to talk about this?"

Lacey blinked, and glanced back at her cameraman, where he stood chatting with a cop. "I was going to do another news spot in a half an hour. Night crew doesn't really have anyone to cover for me…" She rued the idea of leaving her trap unbaited if she left.

KZTB's most colorful personality looked pleadingly at Lacey, and placed a hand on her arm. "I just want to talk. Please, Lacey. I can't do that here. There's so much noise and so many lights it hurts my head," she said. "Come with me? I've got a freezer full of comfort food. Plenty to share."

Lacey felt more compassion, remembering how the woman was there for her at Victor's memorial, and even later that night with a cake. The other thought to pop into her mind was how Greg gloated over having scored with the anchorwoman "a few times." Deborah must have been devastated… But Lacey really didn't want to be distracted from her goal. Not tonight. She was so close to getting answers.

"My car's still down in the garage. I can't really get to it right now." Lacey demurred.

"Mine's out on the street," the other woman said, gesturing. "*Please*, Lacey? Night crew will be fine without you. You were never even *on* it. You don't even work for the station anymore."

Lacey bit her lip. "Can we make it here and back in a half hour?"

Deborah's eyes shone with pain and rejection.

Lacey tried again. "Or, at least before the night is out?"

Deborah turned away and began stalking toward her car. "You could have just said, 'No, Debbie, you can suffer alone.' I could have accepted that."

Lacey sighed inside, and rolled her eyes. "Wait. Deborah. I'll come with you."

"No, don't worry about it."

But Lacey had already caught up, falling in alongside her

staggering coworker. "I'm sorry, Deborah. Now please tell me you have some Ben and Jerry's at home."

Through her tears, the brunette cracked a smile. "Whole gallons." They shared a quiet laugh, then slipped into Deborah's car, waiting for a KZTB van to pass, and then headed into the night.

TWENTY-EIGHT

Deborah's apartment was heaven to the hell of the KZTB basement. Though Lacey still ached all over, she couldn't deny the softness of Deborah's overstuff suede couch, or the way the ivory carpet felt as it massaged her bare feet. The place smelled like a peach orchard, and colorful sconces and lamps provided the perfect accent to the place. Lacey found she was almost jealous of the woman's interior decorating skills.

"I'd offer you chocolate syrup," Deborah said, as she emerged from the kitchen bearing two pints of ice cream, "but…"

Lacey nodded knowingly, and graciously accepted the ice cream from her former coworker, who had since calmed considerably. She pulled off the plastic seal, and took a tentative bite of the stuff, then moaned happily. "Oh, this is *so* good, Deborah."

"Debbie, please. My close friends call me Debbie."

Lacey smiled, more to hide her nerves than anything. "Debbie. Thank you. You were going to tell me about Greg."

Deborah shuddered, and went quiet, then took a large bite of ice cream. A sudden knock at the door caused her to drop the whole pint. She exclaimed, but hurried to the door, and peered through the peephole. Lacey quickly rose, wincing, and made for the kitchen, where she grabbed a dishrag, wetted it, then stepped back into the living room to clean the spill.

"Oh, Lacey," Debbie said, stepping away from the door, "you don't have to do that."

Lacey glanced up at her, then at the door. "It's fine. Who was at the door?"

Deborah frowned. "A couple of men. I think they were religious people or something. I'm not going to answer." As if on cue, the men knocked again. "Act like no one's home," the brunette whispered. "I'll go get something to help you clean." After a moment, Lacey heard footsteps fade away outside, then there was a knock on the door across the stairwell. Before she could think on it further, Deborah was down on her knees beside Lacey, scrubbing at the rich, brown stain. From the corner of her eye, Lacey noticed a small blood stain spreading on the woman's pant leg.

"Debbie?" she said. "What happened? You're hurt?"

Deborah continued to scrub for a moment as if she hadn't heard Lacey. Then, without preamble, said, "I loved Greg. He was a wonderful man." She stood with a small grunt, and turned back toward the kitchen. "I need a towel."

Lacey continued to scrub, but something inside her turned cold. She hadn't seen Victor since she'd been carried away. Her killer was probably already at the KZTB tower, searching for her in vain. Her backup plan even seemed to be coming apart, but she wouldn't let herself think about it. Her once-boss had been murdered, and she had too, and here she was, eating ice cream at the home of someone she barely knew? She needed to get out. She needed to get back to—

A rolled cloth whipped around her neck, and jerked her backward, nearly lifting her fully off the ground. A wicked kick to the back of her knee kept her from rising. Something hard blasted into her head and sent her face first into the carpet. Deborah dropped onto her, knocking the wind out of Lacey, and leaving her stunned. She was pulled up again, her back arching painfully.

"I *loved* Greg Mendoza," Deborah hissed in her ear. "More

than that stupid leech of a wife did. More than *you* did, more than *anyone*." She twisted the garrote tighter. Lacey, still not fully recovered from her ordeal in the basement, found her vision already going gray around the edges. "I *understood* him. He *needed* me."

Lacey couldn't get words out. She clutched at the towel, desperate to clear her airpipe even a little. She thought of Victor, of all he had done for her to keep her alive. She thought of Nainai, for whom she'd been allowed to cheat death to care for. The thought gave her strength, but not enough to do more than halfway topple Deborah.

Deborah quickly righted herself and squeezed tighter, causing Lacey's eyes to bulge. "You thought your little trips to Japan would make him fall in love with you, didn't you?"

Lacey kicked and rolled and squirmed, but every action ate up precious oxygen, and her supply was dwindling twice in the same night. Naked panic started to take over, and, against her will, she felt herself beginning to thrash. But it was useless. The other woman held fast. Lacey felt tears slip down her face, and terror begin to overtake her like it hadn't even in the boiler room when she was sure she was going to die—and actually had. Nainai may never know that her only granddaughter had been murdered just across town. Images of the old woman worrying herself literally to death appeared in Lacey's mind; and for whatever reason, silly guilt arose for not yet having put up a new lucky cat.

"It was worth it, though," Deborah continued. "Following you to Tokyo. Stalking your boyfriend until I found his apartment. He was too dumb to even realize I'd broken in. And that ring he got you? Pathetic. Greg dropped *twenty-two grand* on mine. And then I lost it in the apartment fire. Your boyfriend must have made it fall out of my pocket when he tried fighting back." She barked a short, harsh laugh. "He was so pathetic. And the poison hit him so fast. You at least survived."

"Anyway, you were going to steal my man, and steal my show. I couldn't let that happen. I don't know how you survived that cake. And you got lucky in the basement; I could barely see to shoot. Well, I'll make sure to send you to your cute boyfriend *this* time."

Her voice took on a mock tone of penitence. "It's too bad he had to die. He may have been stupid, but he was a *hunk*." Her voice hardened again. "So was Greg. But if I can't have him, *no one* can. Strangulation may take longer than a gunshot, but it doesn't leave blood stains like the ones I got on my black outfit tonight. How *dare* you shoot me?"

By now, Deborah's words seemed as though they came from the far end of a metal tunnel. Lacey's muscles ached from lack of oxygen, and she felt her resistance growing weaker. She would miss Nainai, even if she got to see Victor again. For a moment, she thought she *did* see him, standing there, worried, but still smiling. Maybe Ms. Tibbits had been wrong about her not dying tonight.

The front door burst open. "Police! Hands in the air!"

At once, the weight was gone from Lacey, and she pulled in a deep, glorious breath that made her head swim. As she lay gasping on the floor, she half heard, half saw Deborah throw herself at the police, clawing, kicking, and screeching. There was a wrestle, but two officers finally got her cuffed, hands and feet.

Light and life returned to Lacey, and she managed to roll awkwardly on to her back, and decided that a good nap might just be in order. If she'd had any doubts about the identity of her killer, Deborah McMahon had now neatly solved those for her.

The unhinged woman kept demanding of the officers, "How could you know? *How*?"

A bruised but beautiful Lacey Ling fingered the hidden mic at her red dress's bust.

Her cameraman hurried in behind the cops. Quickly kneeling at her side, he said, "The sound quality wasn't great, but we got most of what she said. How'd you know you'd need someone following you?"

Lacey merely shook her head, and pointed at her throat,

but she knew, somehow, that the hunch she'd gotten wasn't of her own making. Maybe Victor was still looking out for her after all.

The camera guy nodded, knowingly. "You're lucky we found you. We knocked on several doors before we figured it out. We even hit this one twice." With that, he helped her up, and out toward the waiting police.

In a roundabout way, things worked out. With a little help from Heaven, she had just put three cases of murder to rest.

An unexpected but undeniable feeling washed over her. Somehow, she knew that Victor had finally passed into Heaven. The revelation brought peace. She thought of just how much he'd done for her from even beyond the grave, and it made her smile. Glancing upward, she blew a little kiss. "Thanks, my sweet ex. I'll miss you."

EPILOGUE

"I'll be back in about an hour," Lacey told her grandmother as she slipped on some flats for once, black and sparkly. "I'll get you a lucky cat if it means I have to buy one from the Chinese buffet."

"Oh, good." Nainai was comfortably sitting up in bed, her white hair brushed up into a small bun. "Just don't be too long, like last night. You're always having fun without me!"

Lacey decided against telling her grandmother about all the scary events that unfolded. And in doing so, she also pledged to wear turtlenecks for as long as the purple bruising showed. Nordstrom was having an amazing sale, she wouldn't miss on the way back. "Love you!" she called from the door.

"I love you too, baby girl," Nainai said, and grabbed the remote with her wrinkled fingers.

She turned on the TV. A breaking news story of an illegal imports business being busted was flashing across the screen. By the help of anonymous tips, a couple Japanese men were being arrested, at the center of it all.

"Hmmm." Nainai was interested for about five minutes before she switched the station to another episode of AFV. She especially loved the cat antics: sliding off countertops, swinging from fans, stepping up to big dogs on their hind legs…

She laughed and laughed until tears streamed down her cheeks. Then came the sudden frightening feeling of fragility, of being a woman well into her eighties. Laughter sometimes caused her ribs to ache. Struggling to reposition herself, her chest heaved with the stress of it all. That started up a cough from deep within her lungs. The thought of death came to her, like it had many times before. Was this all normal, old-age stuff? Or would she go to sleep tonight and not wake up?

With the episode wrapping up, she pushed the power button on the remote, letting her head sink into her pillow… when suddenly a very pretty cat was seen stepping across the living room's windowsill. It had gold and black stripes.

Nainai had never seen any cat like that before. Its big round eyes sort of smiled at her with great intelligence shining through them. No, more than that. Wisdom. Great wisdom.

"Hello," Nainai said with a sweet smile. "Are you my new lucky cat?"

The cat sat in the ceramic pose, waving a paw.

Nainai giggled. "You are too cute. Too cute."

To her surprise, the cat spoke. And though its mouth didn't move, it clearly sounded like a refined lady. *It's not your time*, it said.

Nainai's eyes narrowed in seriousness, her smile fading. "When will it be my time?"

The cat smiled, as if holding on to a great secret. *Let's just say Heaven made a promise to someone to extend your stay here.*

"My bones ache, lucky cat. My chest hurts. I'm weak…" Her eyes misted.

The cat teleported to the old woman's bedside. With compassion, it peered at her as if reaching deep inside, talking to her spirit. *You are still needed here on Earth.*

Knowingly, Nainai said, "Lacey."

The cat gave a small nod, then waved a paw over Nainai.

Nainai breathed in deeply, feeling a wave of peace, of all her weakness fading, if for but a moment. She knew it was right to live on. Then she thought of that sweet boyfriend

Lacey once had. "But where's Victor? I haven't seen him in a long time. Doesn't he love my granddaughter? Aren't they going to get married? I told Lacey she needed to stay with him. He would make a great husband. And now he's gone, disappeared, like he never existed."

Can I trust you to keep a secret? the cat said.

"Of course," Nainai said, excited for the response. "Confucius say, 'I'm the best secret-keeper there is!'"

She hasn't seen the last of Victor. He'll be back. He still loves her, always will.

"Oh, that makes me feel much, much better." Nainai gave a closed-mouth smile of pure happiness, shut her eyes, and drifted into a peaceful, deep sleep—the kind where she would awake to her granddaughter greeting her with a big kiss to the forehead, and a ceramic cat in her arms. Huge.

The end.

PHOENIX PRIME

Author Claire Kane and this mystery series became a part of Phoenix Prime.

Phoenix Prime is a Ph.D. level workshop that spans approximately four months. It uses applied industrial psychology to address components of writing, marketing, branding, business and contract issues, productivity, etc. that combine Creative Writing and business perspectives.

The participants create a portfolio to showcase their work alongside students in doctoral programs in several major universities. The objective, in addition to expanding the professional growth of all the participants, is to study the impact of the independent author-publisher on the commercial fiction industry.

ABOUT THE AUTHORS

Claire Kane is an avid reader and writer, who enjoys going on zany adventures with her eccentric mother. She loves classic fashion statements, a good root beer float, and always eats with her mouth closed. And she of course has a weak spot for murder mysteries.

An engineer by day, a writer by night, Stan Crowe has lived more places than he ever imagined he would, and has more children than most imagine they ever will. Author of the collection, "A Comedy of Love," Stan wrote his first book at age five. Of late, Stan and his family have taken to waking up to Arizona sunrises.

Visit www.breezyreads.com for more info.

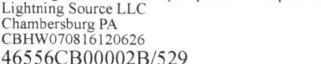